THE TREE OF NOAH

THE TREE OF NOAH

A novel by

REGINALD ASKEW

'A Few, and New Observations upon the book
of Genesis, the most of them Certain, the rest
Probable, all Harmless, Strange, and rarely
heard of before'

Dr Lightfoot, 1682

1971

GEOFFREY BLES · LONDON

Printed in Great Britain
by Cox & Wyman Ltd, Fakenham

CHAPTERS

I

THE TREE OF NOAH

"The problem is that none of us just at the moment is properly capable of deciding anything. Perhaps in a day or two."

"You sound elderly, Japheth."

His mother held in her hand the undertaker's letter. She folded it and unfolded it. It contained his professional advice for the choice of wording on the tomb. No one in the family, thought Japheth, shared the undertaker's taste. He was simply a supplier of funeral provisions who dealt promptly in sacred memories and beloved husbands.

"It is instinctively lamentable. Surely that is right, granny."

"David?"

"Yes, granny."

"What on earth do you mean?"

Her head was still bent over the letter. She was his great-grandmother.

"Noah would have voted for the undertaker."

"How do you know?"

"He would have said that the man knew his job, and that he thoroughly approved of being said to have passed away."

His sister stared. "Shut up. You're appalling."

"Don't you see? Euphemism and a certain, well, fulsomeness are trendy when it comes to funerals. It is because death is vulgar. It is an awful leveller of an event."

"And Noah would be the last, you think, to improve the general taste on such occasions?" said Shem who was listening.

"Don't you think it might be perfectly flat, and in Latin?" said Kezia.

"What? *Noe nongentorum quinquaginta annorum?*"

"David!"

Kezia looked over her glasses at her spouse Japheth. The whole family was crowded somehow into the small sitting-room. It was April. We are ill-assorted, thought Japheth.

Noah had chosen his own burial-place. There was a cemetery which rose upon a hill overlooking the city; all overgrown through neglect, or rather, as Noah noted at once, where green Providence covered things up. The super-intendent apologised.

"We keep doing the paths. The company can't be expected to provide gardeners. They should do their own graves."

"The living, or the departed?"

Noah was on tiptoe.

"It's because everyone's getting cremated, you see."

"I suppose people complain."

"Well, I like a neat cemetery," said the superintendent.

Noah climbed through dark boughs, urns, ivy and retiring memorials, and sat down at the top. He was sitting under a dogwood tree and the city was spread out below. It was a safe spot; the view was good. The tree was in bloom.

Cornus nutallii is the best and the rarest of the dogwoods. It is difficult to establish, but when it is grown, it has no rival. The flower is brown and small as a nut. Each flower is surrounded by bracts like white saucers. The white is not white but brown-white. When the wood is bare of leaves and covered with giant brown-white buttercups, you could imagine anything. You could even imagine special Franciscans coming to squeeze the tree for its brown ink to write on ivory and parchment Alleluia. Under such a tree Noah lay down and measured himself methodically. They would not come often, his descendants. They could come in the spring when the dogwood was aflame, and sit on his stone, and talk over the city, his distant relations.

"It should be quite plain, and say – Here lies Noah who built the Ark."

"I agree."

"But it is customary to include a text."

"It should be quite plain."

"The undertaker's text," said David, "that's a nice text. I like what he's got."

"We know."

"What is it, David?"

"He walked with God."

"Are you . . .?"

"No, I'm not kidding. Anyway it's true, isn't it? Well, the funeral wallah hit on it, and he's the expert."

"Come and sit next to me," said the old lady. The family observed. It was not like her to play the dowager. If she had ever given herself airs it must have been long ago, before any of them knew her, when she was that Cordelia Guppy who married Noah. One can hardly say of the widow, as of the bride, that it is her day. But the family were paying unusual deference to Cordelia their grandmother. She accepted it as a piece of silliness that would wear off. Few people after all were practised at funerals.

"Tell me what you think Noah was like."

"I don't know. I was scared of him."

"Because he was bad-tempered?"

"Oh no! He came from a long time ago, didn't he? But he was quite at home with modern stuff. I mean he wasn't middle-aged. He was more like the chaps at school."

"An overgrown schoolboy?"

"No. But he drank a lot, didn't he?"

"Yes. He died of drink, people will tell you."

"Yes, I know."

"A schoolboyish thing to do, eh? Well, they didn't mention it in church. They hardly could, of course." She found her glasses and unfolded the paper. "They made him sound very grand," said David. She was waiting to read. "*In sacred memory of Noah the Great* – really! D'you think we can? It sounds like an elephant."

"Of singular importance," said Old Shem. There was Old Shem and Young Shem, David's father. It was confusing, for the first five minutes, if at all.

"What, dear?"

"The importance of our decision about what goes on the stone. May not be old Noah, exactly. How we remember him, you know."

Japheth answered his brother. "I can remember him with a mouthful of nails. Remember that?"

"Do I?"

"Well, I can. You can't put that in the inscription even if it's the clearest thing one can remember. Here lies a man with a mouthful of nails. The trouble is we shall all remember him differently."

"Do give me a light, ducky."

Young Shem felt in his pocket. "The boy's got a point. The undertaker's blurb; it's trade stuff, but it's impersonal. There's no call for originality in this department."

"God, it's like choosing wallpaper," said Jemima waving her fag. "What else has the undertaker written us?"

"*In sacred memory of Noah the Great, beloved Husband and Father of the family of Mankind, Protector of the animals, worthy Antediluvian, wise Builder, Master-navigator, Replenisher of the earth after the Flood, this Memorial was erected by his family and the Worshipful Members of the Brewers and Winegrowers Company . . .*"

"Safely above the high-tide mark!"

"Shhh!"

"*He passed away in the Nine Hundred and Fiftieth year of his Age. He Walked With God.*"

"You have a very fine, dignified voice, granny; and I can't think why anyone wants to interrupt." Cordelia returned a smile to Kezia. "Come along. Weren't you at the chauffeur's funeral? Now they were wonderfully sad. But later on, when they got back to the stables, you never heard such laughter floating up to the house. They were real country-folk."

"It's impossible, isn't it, this inscription?"

"Noah would think it mildly funny."

"He would take it seriously."

"I say, he didn't leave any instructions, did he?"

"It would never cross his mind."

They were all joining in now, and it was on the tip of Japheth's tongue to say: "That's what Ham . . ."

"That's what my brother would say," said Old Shem.

They looked to Japheth and he explained. "He means Ham would argue that Noah couldn't care less about epitaphs. But he did, you know."

Ham-Canaan had not been seen at the funeral. It was said he was abroad; it was tricky. The family had never officially disowned him. He was a citizen, not an illegal immigrant. It was just that they had not invited him. If he had turned up, there would have been a place, naturally. It was a state occasion with representatives from all over the world. He was bound to have known. He might have been present in the crowds. Japheth thought that very likely. In the events of the day there had been a sudden awareness of his brother. The procession had left the Abbey in the sunshine, and was a good way towards the hill, when there arose a great sigh from the crowd, and it surged from both sides uncontrollably upon the coffin. The horses rocketed, the police broke, were swept away, and the chief mourners were clinging to the bier as it slid like a chip into the maelstrom. Whether it was homage or fury would never be known, but as the crowd heaved, the coffin shot like a cork from a bottle into the gap ahead. The next moment they were becalmed, and then proceeding as gently as if nothing had happened. They laid Noah to rest among the roots of the blazing dogwood, and returned to the family house. And all the way Japheth thought of the crowd and the accursed Ham-Canaan.

"What an abandoned old gentleman," said Ham-Canaan. For Noah lay on his sagging brass bed in disorder, gurgling with new wine. He chanted the names of the nations, his descendants – Nimrod and Asshur and Uz. He made up the beginnings of limericks and laughed himself insensible. "There was an old party of Uz, who took off his clothes in the bus." Of all the generations of Noah, there was only one man who was not distressed by this intoxication. This was Ham, who accepted his father as Falstaff. He leaned on the bed-rail which had big yellow knobs, and said: "Great snoring pig, is it well?"

The room was full of heavy curtains drawn close. They were not for keeping the draught out, but for keeping the sound of revelry from leaking into the world. "They want to smother you, you fat parrot."

"Recite to me," said Noah. Unsteadily he raised his righteous head. It was a geographical game, a matter of counting the family tree from Somalia to the Aegean. It spread from the Black Sea to the Persian Gulf, from Cyprus to Spain. It was Noah's pride. Egyptian, Hittite, Hamitic and Semitic, Noah's fingers traversed his rumpled counterpane of many colours, following the contours of the known world of his relations.

"Papa, what are you calling this new wine?" But Noah had folded his hands across his bare belly and slept. "Hey, old fellow," said Ham, looking down at the private parts of the wine-giant, "don't you want to get under the sheets?" He arranged the lamps so that the light fell upon the sleeping king. Like a guard of honour, he watched over the friendly naked simplicity of Noah, and noted what a small thing it was that had generated all the people of the earth. He closed the door softly and went down to the library to join the directors' meeting.

"And how is Noah?" enquired the chairman.

"Innocent," said Ham.

"A slight indisposition?"

"No; he's been testing the product, that's all."

The chairman stared. "I imagine we can draw a veil over those proceedings."

"That's a thought," said Ham. "I left him lying on top of the bed. He'll freeze to death."

Shem and Japheth rose as one man, and hastened from the room. When they returned, Ham was exposing the family secret. Japheth resumed his seat and tapped impatiently. "This is not on the agenda."

"It is," retorted Ham happily. "Our celebrated parent has invented wine. Why shouldn't he get tipsy and take off his clothes if he wants to?"

"There's no point in continuing this."

"He makes you nervous, doesn't he?"

"We would rather not discuss this," said Japheth, turning to the chairman.

"You despise him," said Ham.

"We don't. We are sorry for him."

"Why are you so embarrassed?"

The chairman came to the rescue. "Your brothers are naturally concerned. Family matter, eh? I mean Noah is assured of our lasting respect. I think we can say he is held in honour as the ancestor, thought of as the most courageous man who ever lived. No one will deny he brought us safely through the flood."

"He is afloat now," said Ham.

"I beg your pardon," said the chairman.

"You are writing advertisements," said Ham. "Why don't

you face it, that Noah is in his element? All he needs is a head full of wine and he's back on board again.'

The treasurer leant forward. "Are you telling us that he is regularly drunk?"

"He is a buccaneer. He sails on the incoherent waters. He is in league with the deep," Ham added with a flourish.

"Nonsense!" said Shem, "leave it alone. He is very old."

"You see? They want you to imagine that he is a sorry spectacle and a case for a sanatorium. They want to get rid of him. He's a marvellous old man. He drinks and is to be venerated. Can't you understand that? It's part of the product."

"No one in this room is unaware of the greatness of Noah," said Japheth swiftly. "But it is a simple matter of getting the facts straight. I know what you think of your father, Ham. You think he is some sort of sea-god and wine king. The truth is he was no lover of the ocean, and no sailor. He saw the flood only as a universal grave of waters; and he sailed captivated by horror."

"He didn't give a damn for the flood."

Japheth used to sit by Noah on the deck of the Ark, whiling away the time after the rain stopped. The talk was so animated that the greyness of the sky and the emptiness of the great sea round them seemed not to matter.

"I hate it here," he confided in his father.

"I think," said Japheth to the board, "that my father must have drowned many times before the flood was abated."

"He's not on trial, you know," said Ham; "but it is important for the refreshments industry to recognise that he hasn't a care in the world. We ought to publish the fact, not suppress it. This is what is typical of Noah. It's what got us through the flood; a sort of carelessness. And there he is now, snoring like a mountain. It's the same."

"Not a bit. We survived the flood because of his thoroughly business-like preparation of the Ark."

"Whoever compiled such careful inventories?" asked Shem. "You could describe Noah as obsessional in collecting each specimen so patiently. The last thing he was, was careless."

"But that was human anticipation of the emptiness to come. Did you ever see those old tombs opened up, by the Nile? Full of stuff, beautifully stacked and ticked off – what for? Noah was getting ready in the same way for the time that is not our time, for the primeval ocean, where every pattern, landmark, set of tools, and sense of purpose is obliterated. Indeed, to us it seemed like death. To him it was not chaos but rapture. What is the difference now? He has this potent invention, the cup of blessing, and he receives it with exactly the same abandon."

"You won't let it go, will you?"

"Because you won't stop thinking it's disreputable. You have no need to cover up for him."

"I can promise you, Ham, there will be no Dionysian majesty in the morning, and no wine poetry; only an old man with a headache."

Japheth addressed the directors. "His drinking is regrettable, but in the circumstances, understandable. He has never been able to get over the loss of his friends and Wormeaster before the deluge."

"It's called drowning your sorrows."

"We can look after him," explained Japheth.

"They think he is pathetic, you see. That's the trouble," Ham pointed rudely at his brothers. "You wanted him to be an ancient of days whom everyone could be proud of. You would have liked that. It would have helped you to hide from what you really think of him. He is disappointing, isn't he?"

"Very well; if you want to know why our father gives himself up to drink, it is his disappointment. He knows himself. He knows that he is weak and wretched. For all the purging of the universe by the flood, he knows that humanity from which all the rest are descended, is as shameful as ever. He thought the flood could cure this. Indeed, the only justification he could find for the flood was that it would provide a new start for everything afterwards, all the muddle of imperfection in existence swept away. A clean creation – it was a naïve, but satisfying, even noble conception. He was to see a new earth transfigured by rainbows, and a new race all of one family under heaven free from guilt, washed clean. He went into the Ark to be rid of sin. But he carried it with him like a virus. So now he drinks; it is an expression of his disgust and disappointment with himself; and he drinks to excess – to take away the pain."

"We are simply not talking about the same man. It's incredible. Noah's not a failure. He is the man after God's heart. And he is not this simpleton who believed in the flood as a final solution. All right, so he walks unsteadily on his pins – but he walks with God."

"Does he? As long as it worked he could go along with the awful intention of God to drown the world and destroy everything he had known. But it hasn't worked. Life is just the same as ever. He cannot trust God after that."

"You're not with us, Uncle Japheth."

"What is it?" He observed the family peering at him. "I said you're not with us, dear."

There were too many people in the room and he felt oppressed by it and wobbly. "I was thinking about Ham," he said.

"It has been a strenuous day. Still, it's over now."

"I say, it was fascinating, that cemetery. Funny that the old boy should have chosen such a place, with those tremendous weeds growing all over the show," said one of the sons of Shem.

"But it was like him."

"Never seen mare's tail so high. Course, the soil is rich, after all." He laughed all by himself.

"Do you think he was planning to disappear?"

"It was spooky."

"Perhaps he was. After all, he was sly and elusive. He's waiting for the cow-parsley to come and hide him from sight."

"He won't have long to wait!"

"Why should he want to be forgotten?"

"A natural diffidence, my dear. In the end greenstuff covers a multitude of human inadequacies."

Harriet was trembling. The colour of her hair she had inherited from her great grandmother. "How can you? All of you! All day long you have done nothing but say nasty things about Noah!" The tears sprang into her eyes. "I love him. I don't know what I shall do. He is dead, don't you realise? He was the kindest, holiest person there has ever been. What shall we do . . . granny . . . I am so sorry. I didn't mean to cry. I am bitterly sorry. I know they are being joky, really, and don't mean to hurt . . . but I can't bear it any more! Mourn him; please! Mourn him. It is such a weight. I expected it to be all so different; noble . . . as if it would make us all better . . . you know, his dying, it would be a miracle, I thought . . . I am so ashamed." Arms went out to apologise to her grief, but she ran away. It's that rotten little David, thought Kezia, as she went after the child; he started it all. "Harriet? Now where's she got to?"

"Harriet?"

The day had been bright with sharp outlines. The wind was getting up. "It is going to rain," said Cordelia. She was sitting in her wicker-work chair in her own room. "How is Japheth?"

"He's just tired."

"I'm forgetting names. Who was it?"

"Harriet."

"Yes, Harriet. How is she?"

"She will be all right. She takes after you."

Cordelia sat. Families must be allowed to be rude to their father. Goodness knows there would be endless letters written in praise of the patriarch Noah. Dear Noah! He was a legend in his lifetime: and everyone would get it different. It was true he was elusive. He was oblique, in a muddle about everything. If anything was plain, he would look at it through a kaleidoscope. And he was slow. He would have liked to have been efficient.

Japheth's younger son had marched in the procession in full dress kit. He rounded up Harriet in the garden, and stood like a policeman.

"It's the brigadier!" She imitated her mother's voice.

"Yes, Harriet."

"I was hiding. You have outflanked me. That's what you call it, isn't it?"

"Let's say a reconnaissance."

"It's sad, isn't it?" she began more shyly.

"Yes."

"Why were they all so beastly? You don't think like that about Noah, do you? You don't answer, do you?"

"There's no mystery."

"Well, tell me."

"About what?"

"About Noah."

"Noah was a simple man, Harriet. He was chosen for the job he had to do. It was a good choice, as you might expect. He was chosen for the admirable reason that he could take orders without fuss, and then plan and execute the operation effectively. He walked with God. All that means is he understood how things are organised and who were his superiors. The task he was given was clear-cut. He was told what to build, how to build it, and why; and then told to wait for his next instructions. So what did he do? He made his appreciation, took all the factors into consideration, saw what courses were open to him, and formulated his plan. Then it was just a matter of giving his own detailed orders, and of seeing the thing through. He wasn't a genius, or an original thinker, or even a man of vision. He was just highly efficient at reaching decisions in the prescribed manner, and eliminating error."

"It sounds so stiff, like a puppet."

"No. What God does, works. He knows how to delegate; and he selected his man."

"But Noah was ever so original. That's just what he was. He was the only person who wasn't dull."

"Let's think. A really clever man, who was capable of appreciating the situation in full, might be counted on to reject the task as one of impossible absurdity. Noah succeeded because he was only just sufficiently intelligent, because he had morale and leadership, and because he didn't waste time. God counted on him not to let the side down, and he didn't. There's nothing dull about that. The flood was going to be a tight spot, where the stress and fatigue would test even a well-trained man."

"What is a metaphysician?"

"I don't know. You tell me."

"I think it is a person who never makes up his mind."

"Well?"

"Noah was one; least that's what granny said. It's funny, isn't it?"

"Perhaps there are metaphysicians and metaphysicians."

"Well, he was one of the enchanted ones."

"What do you mean?"

"I don't know. He was good at making up stories. Ever so good. He could make things out of paper, too. But the stories were best. I could always see what he was describing. He made everything strange, and more exciting than it is really, I suppose. But I think he knew that things were more beautiful than they seem, and I agree."

"You are talking about wonder, aren't you? It is something simple people have."

"You are trying to get me to think that Noah wasn't original."

"I think originality is a much over-rated quality. I prefer

skill, and a fairly selfless regard for reality. Here come the others. Are you all right, Harriet, or shall I camouflage you?"

"He was a metaphysician, though," she said as she darted across the lawn and back into the house.

"What is a metaphysician?"

Julian and Piers were in the library drinking tea when the brigadier joined them. Piers, diffident and elegant, professed philosophical theology at one of the modern universities.

"Now then, Piers," he said, behaving more like a horse than he needed to, and blushing, "you're just the man I need. What is a metaphysician?"

"The enemy," said Julian promptly. "An eerie, ill-kempt man, a bogus academician, a don without pupils, a liar."

"Piers?"

He shook his head.

"A very minor poet, or disgraceful priest," elaborated Julian; "an instant Socrates, a John the Baptist who frequents cocktail parties, an imaginary general, brigadier."

"No one we know."

"Julian has been reading some antediluvian literature, Coleridge . . ." began Piers.

"Between gulps of opium."

"As a matter of fact, it is interesting what a metaphysician does. It is not as sinister as Julian suggests. It may have a limited use. There is something quirky about it too, but not, I think, criminal. He performs a service to the process of making decisions."

"How?"

"How would you settle the question whether or not the building of the Ark was a selfish act?"

The brigadier thought, and then said: "It wasn't."

"You have settled the question! Would it be possible to convince you that it was?"

"I doubt it."

"But let us suppose that this was a clear possibility raised in a number of minds, that Noah, given every opportunity to warn his compatriots and assist them in making their own lifeboats, kept his mouth shut, and saved his own skin. We, of course, being entirely descended from Noah, feel unwilling to criticise him. You could imagine another survivor, who having swallowed a great deal of the flood, nevertheless managed to float, and who arrived spluttering and indignant where the Ark went aground, very upset that he hadn't been warned or given a berth on the voyage. You could imagine, couldn't you, a court of enquiry set up to investigate Noah and this charge of gross selfishness?"

"Certainly. But Noah would undoubtedly be acquitted."

"How would this verdict be reached?"

"In the usual way with enquiries and courts-martial, on the evidence."

"Difficult to recover?"

"But not impossible. There would be the witness of his family, naturally. And I should expect the animals to be paraded, and to talk up for him."

"Would you allow Noah to be cross-questioned?"

"Yes."

"Plugged in to a lie-detector? Truth drugs? Psychiatrist's report?"

"Yes."

"And we are agreed that the accumulation of evidence by any practical means would be relevant to the settling of the question? I mean, it would be worth digging up some old newspaper predicting the flood to show that people did know about it, or worth measuring the Ark to see if it were the biggest job that anyone could be expected to construct with the labour and materials available at the time?"

"Yes."

"You sound doubtful."

"Well it is clear that the question should never have been raised at all. The very fact of the enquiry suggests that Noah might possibly be guilty."

"Have no doubt. The counsel for the prosecution would make the most of his case. He would present Noah as a mean, private and dangerous man, whose unsmiling selfishness compassed the destruction of humanity!"

"The evidence will satisfy the court."

"All right. Noah is discharged, apologised to, congratulated. But now let us suppose someone who listened to the case, coming up to you and wondering: was it selfishness on Noah's part? What would you do?"

"Go over the evidence with him all over again."

"And if he persisted in asking – was it selfishness?"

"I don't think he would have understood what had taken place. Except the way you put it – was it *selfishness*? with the accent on selfishness – perhaps he is asking something different."

"He is not asking for fresh evidence now, as if what he had heard was doubtful or incomplete. And he is not asking you to remind him of the facts. He wants to know what you mean by selfishness."

"We are all selfish."

"That would be part of the definition, perhaps. Though it is difficult to understand a term which belongs everywhere.

To say we are all selfish clouds the identification of actual selfishness."

"So a metaphysician is a person who asks questions about the meanings of terms."

"Oh no, brigadier. That's a job for lawyers."

"And lexicographers," said Julian.

"Lawyers are paid not only to marshal evidence to settle questions of fact, they are also equipped to supply definitions to settle questions of language. We apply to them with proper confidence to tell us if scientology is a religion, for instance. The point is if the man who is worrying over the question: was Noah being selfish after all? doesn't want more facts, but a workable definition of selfishness, we could supply his need, couldn't we?"

"We could agree on what we meant by selfishness; yes."

"So then the question would be closed?"

"Yes."

"Suppose *now* there is someone who both knows all the facts of the case, and also is satisfied by acceptable definitions of terms like selfishness. Suppose *he* asks the question – was the building of the Ark a selfish act? What is he doing?"

"Going bonkers."

"Julian, you are not to interrupt!"

"You are saying that he is not interested in fresh evidence, or wanting that again, and he is not putting up a doubt about the terminology, and yet he is asking if it was selfish of Noah? I am not clear what he is doing."

"He is simply keeping open a question which all sensible people have settled already."

"He is challenging them to look at what they have decided, to make them take it back."

"This may be the effect of what he does. It is not his motive. It may be that some people got off the bus too hastily, answered the question too summarily. He may make them wary by repeating the question. But let us suppose him perfectly satisfied with their answers, both at the level of evidence, and at the level where grammar is relevant. If he insists now on keeping the question open, he is a metaphysician."

"Short of oxygen, too. I say, brigadier, do have some tea."

Jemima came in. Black suited her. Her hair was silver-white and arranged with old-fashioned elegance. She retained what she had always had, a comfortable, romantic air. She was easily the smartest member of the tribe, and inspired immediate courtly attention in the men.

"Granny is splendid," she said, waving away tea. "She is sitting in her chair so calm and proud and simple. I've always said that when I grow up I want to be like granny! Brigadier, darling, those trews of yours are dashing. How does the army evolve such good taste?"

The brigadier grinned under his moustache. "Interest in morale, Aunt Jemima."

"I must say I expected Noah to have been buried in the Chapel Imperial with all those flags and heraldic stuff, didn't you?"

"These two young men have been insinuating that he was a miserable egoist."

Julian put down the tea-pot on its gleaming tray. "Golly, that's hardly fair."

"It's a little bit right. Could I change my mind, and have some tea after all? What I think really . . ."

They waited for Jemima.

"I think he was a sort of religious aristocrat. The boring thing about most religious people is that they have middle-class attitudes. Noah didn't."

"A snob?"

"Oh no; a gambler."

"A dilettante?"

"If dilettante has something to do with delight, yes!"

"But a fundamental lack of seriousness," said Piers; "one who plays with life, like Adam inventing names for the animals. You could fit superbia into that."

"And a disregard of accuracy," suggested Julian.

Jemima raised an eyebrow. "What do you think it means that he walked with God? What were you going to say, brigadier?"

"I thought it meant he could take orders."

"I think it means that he understood majesty," said Jemima, "if that doesn't sound too pompous."

Cordelia rang, and when he arrived, she asked Burley to move her chair to the window. The sun made deep shadows and light rain was falling on the grass.

"He was quite human, you understand. It was simply that he was raised by an extraordinary and rare vocation."

"If I may be permitted to say so, ma'am, he was a very jolly man."

Beyond the garden, the land rose gently until it came to the hill. Cordelia began her watch, her calm lament, her mourning at her window. Over the tree of Noah a rainbow came and described its arc round the cemetery hill.

"How ludicrous, my dear!" said the poor, old woman staring resolutely forth. A suitable epitaph for Noah would

indeed be difficult to provide. She took up her poem,
beginning:

> *Hic situs est pater tuus, magnus patriarcha*
> *Noe, vir justus, atque perfectus, qui cum Deo*
> *Ambulavit . . .*

II

THE VOCATION OF NOAH

The patron of the living of Wormeaster was an old soldier
who lived close to the sovereign, slept in his armour and ate
pepper, it was said. He was a military banneret, an upright
man and ferociously successful. Noah sulked in his presence.

"Now you were too young to serve in the war. That's not
your fault. That's your mother's fault."

How do you deal with playful aggression? Noah did not
know if it would be right to stamp his feet and shout "Sir!"
or bristle up and challenge him to a duel. It was unfair.
He was sitting on the man's sofa, next to the archdeacon,
with a cup of tea which was going cold in one hand and a
small piece of toast in the other.

"You've got nothing on your toast. Have some of this,
what's it called, cad's paste?"

"Gentleman's relish." Noah was going white and
dull.

"Cad's paste." He pulled his glasses down his nose and
inspected the candidate with great impertinence and shrewd-
ness. "It says you have written a piece on the Epideixis of
Irenaeus. Who's he?"

The archdeacon felt himself included in this salvo and
surrendered a grin like a piano.

"A famous exegete, a biblical scholar; a dogged man."

"There's glebe at Wormeaster. You a farmer?"

His wife, Lady Hittite, was nursing a dog in her lap. She too had won all her battles. "We have two thousand acres, haven't we, little darling?"

"Soldiers make the best farmers, archdeacon."

The archdeacon had been briefed to sell this parcel of goods. He felt his way. "His father, sir, now he served in the brigade, and settled in the country." He leant forward to receive cake. He was actually wearing his medals, and they clinked. "I knew him."

"You're not married."

Poor Noah.

"Tricky; they feel safer with a man who's married."

"Much safer," she agreed, hugging the doggie. "Do you like village people, reverend? Of course, you read books. How boring!" she said it without a trace of malice.

The archdeacon looked helplessly at Noah. "We all get married one day. Of course the living has been vacant for some time. It would suit a man who was married, or about to get married."

"Did you know the chaplain's married? Such a nice girl!" The dog wagged a paw. "They're on leave, aren't they? That's right. Isn't it a pity that the right jobs don't always come up at the right time?"

"We do our best, ma'am."

"Of course, I don't know how they would manage on chaplain's pay. It's fortunate that they have money."

"I'm not saying that it's a rich living," the soldier explained to Noah. Indeed it was not. Long, long ago it had counted as the largest prebend of the cathedral, and the holder of the stall a magnate. The prebendal house still stood under

Wormeaster Sleight with a stone cross carved in the finial of the roof. Now it was a farm labourer's cottage.

"But such tradition, dear. I think tradition so important, don't you? So rich in tradition!"

In the cathedral guide Noah had noticed an inscription in Lombardic capitals. He went to look for it. It said:

> Pvr l'alme Johan
> De Warmestre Priez:
> Et treize jovrs de

The last line of the verse had never been cut. It had been the vocation of Canon John of Wormeaster to die of the plague. The stonemason had sneezed and followed him. In one of the side-chapels lay the stone effigy of a tonsured priest, with a subtle air of after-lunch contentment in the face. He slept smiling. Him no one expected to have been married, to have fought in the wars, or to have eschewed learning.

"Tradition is always incomplete," said Noah. "That's why it's difficult to sweep away."

"I don't think they would relish your changing anything."

"No, ma'am."

"I think Noah means that tradition is enduring, and reliable," said the archdeacon, "standing firm above the waters of time."

"Oh, I like that," she said. "Is that what you meant?"

"I meant tradition is something that is handed over, and depends altogether on the disposition of those who receive it. Their freedom renders the tradition incomplete. Com-

c

plete freedom brings tradition to an end. That is why the
New Testament speaks of a new creation . . . and why St.
Matthew, who is very conscious of tradition, describes the
freedom of Jesus not as destroying but perfecting it."

"Now the people of Wormeaster," replied the soldier,
"are simple people. What they want is plain teaching
straight from the shoulder. As I've always said, there are
three things: truthfulness, integrity, and moral courage!"

The archdeacon straightened his back. Lady Hittite smiled
triumphantly at Noah. He had hoped for the incumbency of
little Wormeaster, but there was a dog in the manger. The
eyes of the soldier were fastened upon him. In a gesture of
defeat Noah tried to make friends with the dog.

"So you like animals, reverend?"

"Yes, ma'am." He put out his hand to stroke the animal
in her lap.

"He will bite you!" she announced with glee.

Noah threaded his way through the streets. He was lost
now. He thought he had a vocation, but he was too dismally
proud to be vetted. If the guardian of Wormeaster had asked
him, will you be a watchman of the Lord, will you pre-
monish and provide for the villagers, and seek for Christ's
children who are in the midst of this naughty world, will you
be studious in reading and learning the Scriptures, set aside
worldly cares, and ripen in your ministry? he would not have
concealed his ardour, but would willingly have kissed the
hilts of the old man's sword. But they were looking for a
clergyman armed with a wife, and a leg full of shrapnel, a
pastor untroubled by theology who spoke their language.
Were they not right? How is a vocation different from the

sum of other people's expectations? How can God tell you to serve him in Wormeaster unless the patron approves?

Noah had been quite clear about it. He could do the job; he was trained for it, thoroughly. He was not mistaken. Health, stamina and common sense were what was wanted for a start. Then generosity, fidelity to prayer, detachment, and a taste for poverty were needed. Then delight, the ability to make peace, to suffer, to inspire, to preach mercy, were necessary skills. He was ready to embrace the parishioners of Wormeaster, to love them, to praise them, to lift up their hearts, and to mend his faults. But he did not feel content to be ill-thought of in the soldier's drawing-room. Kyrie eleison! He had to start all over again.

He crossed the park. There was a fine haze in every tree before the buds open. The pale broom *kewensis* was flowering in profusion. But in Wormeaster it was already hay harvest when news came of their vicar. They had dusted the little wooden church and made it nice for Ascension Day. The rural dean from Oldbury Warren had obliged with services in the interregnum. He forgot to put out the candles in the corona luci above the altar, and that night Wormeaster Church was burned to the ground.

From his school window, Mr Peris Morgan was used to surveying the yard, the lavatories, and the school lane. The lane was full of big leaves from the Indian bean which grew in the headmaster's garden. Catalpa leaves are suitable material for a Nature Table. The name lends distinction. Children over many years had discovered that oak and sycamore were good, but that the name catalpa registered you as a botanist. As Noah came down the lane and across the wet schoolyard,

Mr Peris Morgan decided that he was too new even to be the new vicar. A scholar of ability, he had heard, of good family and of private means. He pursed his lips. The headmaster's study was too small. He went out therefore to defend the entire territory, and stood in the entrance of Wormeaster school like a ticket-collector. All services were held in the school.

"The boys and girls are going to sing to you. It is an important day for us." Noah breathed the air of school paint and wet macintoshes. He was at home in Irenaeus Against Heresies, and his world contracted. If he kept this obscure information from the children, appropriately, he would be speechless. Mr. Morgan led the way into the assembly hall. And now he was explaining the importance of the day in a louder voice. Mr Peris Morgan had a florid face, but his voice was extremely clear, admirable, and Welsh. At one nod, half the school sat down. The rest emerged neatly and formed themselves, smallest in the front, into a choir on the teachers' platform. The headmaster watched with the closest attention. Then he placed himself at one side of their ranks, and bent his knees as if to spring. When he was satisfied that he had secured in his crouch the stillness of the entire hall, he bounded; and the choir sang.

Beatus, beatus vir! Noah was rooted to the spot. He had expected, observing the carefully rehearsed solemnity of the children's movements, something unmusical and pat. Instead the stupendous polyphony of Monteverdi filled the school and flowed out into the autumn. The verve and accuracy of the choir, their happiness, sprang upon him. Never had there been such a welcome. He looked up full of plans. Towards the back, a little taller than the rest, was a young woman

with a pale face and a lot of dark red hair. Her chin was
raised on a long neck. They were all singing like nightingales.
He was looking at Cordelia Guppy for the first time. Miss
Guppy taught history at Wormeaster Church school.
Beatus, beatus vir!

She crossed the uneven cobbles in Glebe lane and found
Noah in the stables, dressing his horses.

"First the curry comb; then dust, then rub with the brush,
then dust and rub with wet hands. After that, a clean wipe
with a woollen cloth, then a linen cloth; and lastly comb
down his mane and tail," instructed Noah.

"Are they really your horses?"

"He is so fine, isn't he, that he could only belong to himself. See how small the ears are, thin and sharp and carried
well. And the face lean and bony, his forehead swelling out-
wards, and the feather of his face, here, set fairly high above
his eyes."

"Such eyes, round, black and shining."

"As they should be. They stand out from his head. The
cheekbones are lean, and the space between them wide, and
free from knots, or what my father used to call kernels. The
nostrils are wide and dry. That's right. The snip of his nose
is marked white. The muzzle's not too big. It's a deep mouth,
and lips shut tight. Come on, let's see; perfect teeth, and the
tushes small and sharp."

Noah patted him down. "Broad-breasted beast, the fore-
thighs to the knees firm and sinewy without any swelling . . .
the knees are close-knit, and no scars. From the knees to the
pasterns his legs are clean, and nervous. The pasterns are not
too long; and look how he treads on them."

"Black hoofs; aren't they smooth?"

"They're quite long really."

Cordelia bent forward, her hair hiding her face. Noah had stood many times on the school platform and had preached to Cordelia Guppy. That is to say he had preached to her shining head. He had addressed the dark red hair with such evangelical fervour that he became known as a man of God.

"His neck is like an arch; and his head, when he stands naturally, falls perpendicularly to the ground."

"What is it, Noah?"

"The mare is fine too; large sparkling eyes, and a great body so that the foal may have room enough to lie . . ."

"What is it all for?"

"For the Ark."

"You don't believe all that, do you?"

It seemed to Noah that she had never looked more beautiful. This light girl was destroying him.

"You are staring, Noah."

"It is true, whether anybody believes it or not."

"It's just a myth. The children are saying that you are building a houseboat. Noah! I must say; what a joke!"

"There's going to be a flood. And we have no church."

Cordelia turned her attention to the close, sleek coat of the horse she was grooming. Then she pointed with the curry comb. "Even if there were, it would be no use making a houseboat."

"Why not?"

"If you believe in God, then you will have to believe that his will is almighty."

"Yes?"

"So according to his will, what will happen, will happen.

In other words, if it's true there's going to be a flood, it's also true that it won't be prevented."

"Well?"

"Well, that leaves two possibilities. Either Noah will get drowned, or he won't. If he will not drown, making a life-boat will just be a waste of time. And if he will die in the flood, the houseboat won't save him, will it? So it's not much use, Noah, when you come to think of it."

He leaned on the gentle mare. "I don't suppose we shall ever make things different from what they will be. But in fact we often make them other than they would have been."

"What d'you mean? Let us suppose for the sake of argument that you will not be drowned. Well, if it is a fact that you will not be drowned, it must remain a fact, whether or not it is also a fact that you finish building the Ark in time."

"If I'm not going to die by drowning, is it true already? I mean, are there any facts about the future? For instance, it might rain tomorrow. But can you be certain of that? It's true that there are people in the village who can look at the sky and be pretty confident about their predictions of what's going to happen to the weather. But they are bound to make more of the evidence than it warrants."

"You are being unnecessarily cautious now. Of course you can pretend that no proposition is certain unless it's either a tautology, or capable of being verified by present experience. If you want to take that line, you would have to say that it's quite uncertain that there will be any tomorrow, let alone whether it will be raining. Things aren't that queer, are they?"

"Well, I admit that if it wasn't perfectly certain to me that there would be a tomorrow, I should hesitate to tidy up one more horse."

"There!"

"Still, the future is different from the present and the past. Do you know that poem, which goes:

> They ate, they drank, they bought, they sold,
> They planted and they builded.
> They ate, they drank, they bought, they sold,
> And one day it rained fire and brimstone . . ."

" . . . from heaven, and killed the lot!"

"Well, that's what makes the future different from the past, Miss Guppy. Nothing can stop the facts of the past from being what they are. But future events are still at sea and in danger of shipwrack."

"Don't you say shipwreck?"

"You may. Past events are safely home in port. But the future, well . . ."

"But that's my point. Hasn't God got the future quite as safe and determined as you feel about the past? Is he almighty; or is he nervous and risky? Surely, if God is determined to save Noah and drown the rest of the world in a flood, won't it be just an example of the predestinate will and foreknowledge of God?"

"It's no good being a determinist."

"I'm not."

"You are."

"Well, perhaps you are bound to if you take the will of God seriously."

"Determinism is self-defeating. All one has to ask a determinist is what makes him one. For we shouldn't accept any hypothesis unless it can be reasonably supported. But determinism can't be reasonably supported. It can only be determinedly supported."

"That sounds frightfully glib."

He had spoilt it. "You mentioned predestination. I think predestination refers to the past. It has to do with a person looking back, and recognising everything that has brought him to the moment where he stands in time, and it makes him glad."

"Well at this moment of time, I shouldn't be in this stable. I'm going to be late." She ran down the school lane. At the corner she stopped and turned and her cold red hair swirled behind her. She waved with both arms above her head. So she had forgiven him. Noah burst into his study and sat before his sermon in the most exquisite solitude, and with his hands still full of the perfume of horses.

The Diocesan Review Board for the Care of Churches favoured a modest building in common brick with an asbestos roof, and the architect was keen to leave the RSJs of the roofspan exposed, to have north lights, and to give a general feeling of what he called a workshop for liturgy.

"Won't it feel raw?"

"That's right; a sense of plain engineering. After all, worship must find its technological expression. Fibreglass would be better than brick, of course. But the Board, you see, are understandably conservative."

"It's like a shed."

"Well, it's a matter of money, really, isn't it? But I think that you'll find the asymmetrical treatment of the roofs, with these contrasting steep angles, very exciting. I think a

mixture of experiment and aspiration on a limited budget is
what we're after."

Noah stared at the neat elevations. He imagined the
poverty of the roofs, apron flashings and barge-boards after
a few years' weather.

"Isn't asbestos-cement a very dead material?"

"It can be painted," the architect explained kindly. He had
been through this a number of times. "There's aluminium or
copper; but can you afford it? What is needed in these
matters is a practical vision. I can imagine that Wormeaster
thinks of itself in old-fashioned terms. But it is being drawn
into an industrial society. There will be the motorway and
the week-enders. Some of them will pretend to be small-
holders. But well-designed tower flats is what they really
need. Otherwise you're just going to get floods of caravans
and chalets. This church building, though inexpensive, and
there is something to be said for apostolic simplicity – you
are the theologian – is a building which will tone in with the
new environment in a forward-looking way."

"If there's going to be a flood," said Noah. "I would like
a church that can float."

The architect grinned. "Precisely!" They shook hands, and
on his way out Noah was given a photo-printed copy of
'Tomorrow: God's Space in Industry and Affluence.'

Noah's ally in the Parochial Church Council turned out to
be Mr Peris Morgan. The meeting, which had become
lowered and sickly in its deliberations about money, now
began to brighten when the cheapness of the scheme was
argued. Mr Morgan could wait no longer. He straightened
his springy knees. "The diocese wants to build you a gar-
ridge! What you should ask yourself is could you sing in it?

Does it make you sing? The church is the place which should be ready for life, for creation. This is a hangar! It is for dislocated machinery! There is no resonance here, and no growth. Let me remind you of Solomon's temple. That was a small job too. But Solomon built the house out of the forests of Lebanon. Hiram king of Tyre floated him down cedar trees and fir trees; and there were posts of olive, and doors of olive tree carved with open flowers. And so they could all stand there and say: Lift up your heads ye everlasting Doors!"

"And how long did that take, Mr Morgan?"

"It took seven years." He meant business.

"We've always had a wooden church, Mr Morgan." Tradition was reasserting itself shyly. "And I always thought the Temple was built of stone. Would it have split oak shingles on the roof, then, like old Wormeaster?"

The Welshman opened his hands. "It was full of psalms and pomegranates like smoke!"

Noah looked round the meeting. Under her fierce hair Miss Guppy gazed steadily at the headmaster with such admiration, that when she caught Noah's eye, she hid.

"It shall be made all of wood," Noah concluded. "And if it takes us six hundred years, we shall do it ourselves."

A farmer took him aside at the door. "There's timber in my top wood, sir, you can have. You'll need horses, mind, to drag it."

Cordelia said: "The headmaster likes you. But I was wondering about Solomon. I shouldn't be at all surprised if his taste wasn't much more like the Festival of Britain than Mr Peris Morgan imagines. Do you think the diocese will fight?"

"Until it rains."

Noah went to bed and dreamed of the great dark church, resinous, thicketed with timber. He climbed into the roof space to feel the principal rafters. The ridge boards were like the keel of an upturned boat. Out of the keel started stem and sternpost, frame, keelson and futtocks curving round to the wall plates of the church like the skeleton of a beast. Where the ribs of the Ark bent round he would place the thickest planking, to make the whole ship bulge in a seaworthy fashion. He stepped from truss to truss on the beams looking down into the hold of the nave where the animals would be. The wooden pillars rose like a forest and nothing stirred on the floor. His voice echoed through the wood. "I am Noah, maker and master mariner." And so he hung, his own figure-head, over the tide of a celestial ocean. Making the Ark was such continuous satisfaction to him, that when he brooded thus over the face of the waters, or when he rested from working the gopherwood, he reflected that even if there were to be no flood at all, he would have wanted to be the maker of Saint Ark.

"You have a vocation, for sure," said Cordelia, when she came to see how the church was getting on. "I suppose I should congratulate you. What is it like?"

"What?"

"Having God speak to you, receiving instructions from God."

Noah had a mouthful of nails. He looked wooden, sitting cross-legged like a puppet. Cordelia went on: "That's what it was, wasn't it?"

He took out the nails. "All I know is that I have such

pleasure in this work, that even if the Lord had not invited me . . ."

"Instructed you."

"Instructed me, to build an Ark of such and such dimensions, and even if there were not the smallest chance of a flood, I would have wanted to be the builder."

"Ah!"

"What d'you mean – ah? I'm trying to explain what a vocation is. It is to love God and do what you really want."

"So he didn't speak to you?"

"You used the word vocation. What did you mean by it? Someone has a vocation if God calls him."

"Specially if it's to be full-time religious work," she said.

"All right. My job is usually called a vocation. There are other callings, like nursing and teaching which get the same label. But what about a navvy on a building site? Is that a vocation? Would working in a cigarette factory count? Or being somebody's bookmaker? If you sat all day in a typing pool, but in the evenings put your skill and energy into dress-designing, someone would be sure to compliment you on your sewing by saying: You've missed your vocation. So what is it? I'll tell you the first thing it is. Do you remember the day I came to the school? Wasn't that a long time ago?"

"Yes; we sang *Beatus vir*."

"That choir has a vocation. And by that I don't mean anything particularly pious. They sing for the joy of it. It's a motive we all have; doing things for the love of doing them."

"That's not a religious explanation. Don't misunderstand me. I admire what you're doing. But you have a sense of being in league with God, haven't you?"

"Yes."

"I would like to suggest an alternative account. In the first place, construction, or any creative activity like church-building or ship-building, is marvellous, if you like, holy. Inventiveness and dexterity inspire awe. What is more, building the way you are doing is a recipe not just for sanity but for a sort of beatitude. The most elementary craftsman feels the same. But they are simply superlatives, these religious words – awful, holy, beatific. To catch the ecstasy one needs adjectives in the superlative. I can remember typing out the specification for the timber merchant. What was it? All timbers to be of good quality, sound, bright, and free from shakes, large loose or dead knots, wany edges, and to be properly seasoned. It's delicious. My heart leaps up when I behold the foremost cant-timbers of the Ark, and all that acacia-wood. But there is no need to speak literally of divine building instructions, Noah."

"You are saying that what I take for the voice of God is really my own job-satisfaction in building, and my preference for wood rather than asbestos? Well, it's true – as far as it goes. But it doesn't really explain things."

"In your case it's not only that. There's this queer sense of purpose. Making something well is exciting enough, but you seem to be making it against a foreseeable future, as if you were omniscient, as if you expect a calamity in which a wise man will need more than an umbrella."

"A sense of eschatology?"

"You can call it what you like. But it's human. There is no need to describe our capacity to anticipate the future as if we had a supernatural source of information. If what you are preparing is an intelligent piece of insurance, wouldn't it be enough to call it prudent and sharp-sighted of you?"

"What is the difference between doing what I honestly think I ought to do, and doing what God commands?"

"Precisely!"

"Is it the same thing, Cordelia? It may look the same. Is doing what I think will turn out for the best, and doing what God wants, the same?"

"Anyway you are not sure it will turn out for the best."

"What d'you mean?"

"This eschatology stuff – it makes you afraid. You have a foreboding about the pressure of things, population or something, that is going to bring everything to an end. That's why you drag God in."

"When God made all things in the beginning," said Noah, "he divided the waters from the waters. To destroy creation he will let go. Creation will sink in the clashing deep; and in such a space, featureless and terrible, I shall have to navigate my craft."

"Speed, bonny boat! It is your insignificance that troubles you, isn't it? When you are just a speck among the galaxies, lost among the mountains and water-spouts, no wonder you might wish yourself in touch with some almighty and pervasive spirit. But what you would mistakenly call trust in God in such moments, I should prefer to describe as plain nerve – a sort of heroic impudence, or maybe it's insensitivity – in face of the emptiness of the universe."

"I'm not responsible for the order or the design of the universe, you know. And I'm not responsible for its wildness."

"But you do feel responsible. I know, you are contemplating a sort of rescue operation – for the horses at least, but you would like to take with you select pairs of the entire fauna. As if you have been put in charge of the animals! But you haven't. You are simply the latest feature of evolution. Caring for your inferiors is just a case of *noblesse oblige*. You are not accountable to anyone for the way you treat other forms of life. You are nobody's steward or conservation agent. If you are kind to animals, it is not because you are likely to meet your Employer in the half-light and cool of the day, but because it is right to be loving to the animals and that's all."

"So you think my vocation is a mixture, really, of a pleasure in construction and precautions for the future and fear of the universe and this zoological concern?"

"Yes."

"You are very kind. I thought you would say I was doing it all because I hated people, and would do anything to depart from an intolerable civilisation, and didn't care if everything were swept away in a universal grave of waters."

Noah was joining the boards by the method of rebate, groove and tongue. "It's a secret joint, bit expensive, but it ought to keep the water out. Your wish to translate God's commands to me into a collection of my desires and fears indicates that you want to keep things under control. What I said at the beginning was that doing God's work was actually a pleasure. You immediately seized on this to replace the bewildering name of God with pleasure. I wish you felt more free."

"How?" A nail went in crooked; he wrenched it out.

"One of the purposes of religious language is to help you

to dislodge yourself from what has become habitual and to see everything that was familiar for the first time. The point about talking of a vocation is that it draws attention to some imperfectly recognised feature of everyday experience. This is a nuisance because it involves you in a departure from everything you had taken for granted as secure."

As if to emphasise what he was saying, he banged upon the well-joined deck. "I didn't expect to be doing this job, you know. I thought I had lost it at the interview. They were looking for something quite different. And the Review Board did not exactly have this building in mind. When I said I thought I wanted a church that could float, the architect was amused. You need not think of a vocation as a very direct thing, as if the voice of God were undeniable and clear. It is rather indirect and accompanied by anguish."

"But it did all work out for you."

"Nothing can separate us from the love of God."

"Then what is 'the imperfectly recognised feature of everyday experience'?"

"It is nothing else but the freedom of God."

"You'll have to explain."

"I'm preaching about it on Sunday," said Noah.

III

NOAH'S DISCOURAGEMENT

The school cloakroom was used as a vestry. A farmer called Coombes, whose children were in the choir, carried the cross. Noah waited by his side.

"I don't suppose your mother will like this wet weather?"

Coombes thought a long time.

"No," he said, "'tis the hot weather will kill she." How slowly and simply he spoke!

Noah realised that he had not got their speed yet, or thinking as they thought. He loved the country tempo, but had not achieved it. His sermon now filled him with trepidation. It was too late to do anything about it. They filed into the school hall, and when the time came, he said:

"Now, then, to preach a green sort of sermon, and to let it fall into the country soil which people have got at the bottom of their hearts, with the hope that it might grow things.

"This is the argument. It is about praying – because Rogation Sunday means a Sunday for asking prayers, and traditionally a time for blessing the crops, a prayer for employment, daily bread and economic security. Prayer is the chief clue to what a person believes. What you believe about prayer is a sign of what you believe about God.

"But asking him for things is difficult for those whose overriding belief about God is that he is unchanging. What chance is there of getting an immovable, all-knowing God to change the course of events, or to alter his unalterable will in our favour? If that is how you see it, then you have to be persuaded that the most important fact about God is that he is free. If a man comes to recognise that God is free, really free, from that moment, and perhaps for the first time in his life, he can pray, and pray believing.

"The freedom of God is at the back of what we mean when we call him Creator. The freedom of God is what rescues you also. It rescues you, incidentally, out of the hands of the church and the preacher. It is what allows everything that is within you, undomesticated and of infinite promise, everything you would call your wildest hopes, to stand before God and recognise its source.

"How can I persuade you that God is free? We have to reckon with the fertility of God, with a ruthless, terrible will to make life and to make it immodestly. Dare you ask for such spring tides, and such carnal momentum? But who is not aware of this wild, immoral generosity in God? Is it not he who would fill every farm saucer with a forest of mustard and cress? He has an uncontrollable green nature. He is like the mystery of the economy which the economists cannot pin down. The returning dream of an insecure people is a stable economy with calm annual growth and steadily increasing prosperity. This is just the wistfulness of politicians. Life is not so. That is what makes it life.

"But God is even more life, even more insecure, even more free. He is alarmingly free. He is free enough to be at home in the universe even if it were all chaos. We can only do with order. But in disorder he is not lost, nor unable to get a bearing for the line of his plough.

"If a man believes that God is free, and especially free from him, he can pray for the first time. To the fixed and unchanging and eternal, how can he pray? What is fixed and unchanging is like those big stone faces upon the islands in the Pacific Ocean. But to the one who is free, free from all constraints, free from all patterns and rules of procedure, free from any habit and from all obligations, to the one who is not hindered from taking steps, and taking action, to that one a man can actually pray. In that one there is such an abundance of freedom, such a fountain of possibilities, that the psalmist says down the echoing place: With thee is the well of life.

"Do you remember what Jesus says in the fourth gospel when he sat by the well talking with such impudent freedom to a strange girl? Look up the gossip between that man and that woman at the well. No time now! It is a pagan picture of God. Or rather, it is at least a pagan picture, and a typical decoration for a jug. What would pagans have drawn on the belly of the jug? A girl between an avenue of laurels, with her Greek profile and no clothes on, going like the wind towards the city. "Come and see," she cries, "a man who told me all that I ever! Can this be a spring of water welling up to eternal life?"

"It is the freedom of Jesus, and the swift feet of the woman, which shows God incarnate in the story. It creates hope in me also, wild hope that when I ask for daily bread, he actually can and will. It becomes both a prayer for the crops, for employment, and for economic security, and also for the holy food, for the coming of the kingdom, of which this eucharist is a token."

The trouble is, thought Noah, as he accepted the eucharist,

it was too neat. The preacher has to resemble the message. A sermon about mercy should itself be ungrudging and for-giving; a sermon about Jesus should be captivatingly authoritative; about the sabbath's rest should be full of a blessed stillness; about Easter should be itself miraculous. And a sermon about the freedom of God should be much looser. It should be like children running out of school. It should have the wind in it when the leaves are blown. It should make people say: Why hop ye so, ye high hills? There should be something unconstructed about the sermon, an antinomian air. The freedom of God is a very disturbing mystery. If the preacher had believed it, he would have con-veyed it. Noah thanked God for the passion and resurrection of Christ that makes all things well, and rightly and duly ad-ministered the sacrament.

Perhaps the wildness of God did infect their gentle lives. Perhaps under all those seemly hats there was a divine con-fusion. Perhaps they approached the Rogation season with a simplicity and country understanding which had no need of formal theology. There were certainly hands there which exposed their covenant with the soil, blunt and practical hands, a horny place for the host to lie. And there was Cordelia with her smooth red hair. Open thy mouth, and I will fill it with honey!

It was disgraceful, thought Noah, to offer the chalice as if it were a proposal of marriage. We are both guests of the generosity of Christ. Yet just as there is inexplicable splen-dour in the marriage feast at Cana of Galilee and the miracle of spring water made golden, so the inarticulate Noah stood before the kneeling girl in that plain schoolroom and needed no sharper epiphany than the devotion of that communicant.

All she needs to have is a cold, for the sun to go in, and the wine to run out, for us to realise that Noah is too happy, and that the earth is no vehicle for the transcendent glory. But it is too late, and it is springtime, and people are asking God wild things.

There was no activity in the churchyard. "Come in," said Noah softly. He was resting up beside the derelict church in a workman's shelter. The wind flapped the loose end of a tarpaulin. It surprised Cordelia to see how withered his face looked.

"It's this dust," said Noah moving up to make room. "I'm as dry as a bone." He stamped his feet as if to shake them free of a fine deposit.

"You haven't been working," observed the visitor directly.

"I've been standing here like a miller, sailing my arms round and round."

"It is very daring to stop work, Noah!"

"Do you think you can sniff the flood coming, then?" In his mind's eye, he saw the yellow torrent pouring slackly across the dry ground. He saw it lick the Ark and toss the whole timber yard into flotsam. "It's like a skeleton and not like a church at all. It looks as if it hauled itself across the plain with its tongue hanging out, and died of drought just there."

Besides the carpenter's tools, nails, pots of glue, there were on the bench and stacked on the floor a great many books. Cordelia noticed *Annales Veteris Testamenti* by J. Ussher and a book by J. Lightfoot D.D. 1682 entitled, *A Few, and New Observations upon the book of Genesis the most of them Certain, the rest Probable, all Harmless, Strange, and rarely heard of before.* There was *A description of the East and some other countries,* Vol 2, by R. Pococke 1764 and John Hutchinson's *Moses's Principia.* She picked up the *Historie of the World* by Ralegh which lay open:

" '... by the gravest Astrologian it was observed that in the year 1524 there should happen the like conjunction as at Noah's Floud; than which ... there was never a more faire. dry and seasonable year." How priceless! Is this what you've been reading?" She put it down, and started looking at *A hyve full of hunneye* by William Hunnis, London 1578. "What has stopped you working, Noah?"

"There's the problem of getting all the animals in."

"It doesn't worry you, does it?"

"Supplies as well; it's a very famous problem. Listen to this." Noah ferreted through his library until he found the *Commentary upon the Historical Books of the Old Testament* by Patrick, Bishop of Ely. "Someone had urged the objection that 'there being so many sorts of living Creatures, that they could not possibly be crowded into the Ark, together with Food sufficient for them. But such Persons never distinctly considered such things as these. FIRST, That all those that could live in the Water are excepted: and so can several Creatures besides Fishes. SECONDLY, That of the Species of Beasts, including also Serpents, there are not certainly known and described above an hundred and fifty (as Mr. Ray hath observed) and the Number of Birds about five hundred. THIRDLY, That there are but a few Species of very vast Creatures, such as Elephants, Horses &c. And, FOURTHLY, That Birds generally are of so small a bulk, that they take up but a little room. And, FIFTHLY, That if we suppose creeping Insects ought to be included, they take up less, tho' very numerous. And, LASTLY, That less Provision would serve them all, when they were shut up close, and did not spend themselves by Motion; and besides, were in a continual confused Agitation which pall'd their Appetites. From all which, and many more Considerations, it is easy to demonstrate that there was more than room enough . . .' Not very convincing, is it?"

"Let me look. It's heavenly; and didn't they have gorgeous print? Of course the trouble is this chap has got the problem the wrong way round. What is the Ark? It is by definition that which has room for all the animals. If it didn't have enough room, it wouldn't be the Ark. Don't you agree?"

"Silly."

"Not at all. If the passenger list includes everything that is an animal, if it includes the name of every animal, anything that doesn't fit in can't be an animal, can it?"

"All right, if the Ark is by definition that which comprises all living things, it leaves the question whether this that I am doing is the Ark or not. It may be a logical mistake to doubt the capacity of the Ark; what is open to doubt is whether this is the real Ark! That is why I have stopped working."

Cordelia put her head in her hands and looked out at the building. It didn't look like a skeleton. There was scaffolding, yes, but it looked already like a forest of telegraph poles that was ready to vault itself naturally under its own roof.

"What you want me to say is that the real Ark is a church, don't you?"

"No, but I like arguing with you." It was true, but it was

not the whole truth. He wanted to kiss her. "You were saying that you can't ask an *a priori* Ark questions of contin-
gency."

"I'll tell you one thing, Noah. These books you have been
burrowing in – if you laid them all end to end, they would
sink like a stone."

"What if the Ark were a church?"

"If it were, you wouldn't stop building. If the church is
the vessel by which all mankind is to be saved, you wouldn't
stop to wonder if everyone was able to get on board.
Millions of people are nowhere near getting on board. That
doesn't alter the instructions to the builders. The instructions
are: Go and baptise all nations. No, you have stopped because
you don't believe that there's going to be a flood."

"It's too dry," he said. "The timber seems so parched that
I think the next thing it will do is burst into flames."

"This is going to be a much nicer church than the last
one."

"I have been waiting for rain. But if it came now it would
not slake the thirst of this desert. If it came now, my timbers
would gulp it in, and bud, and put on their leaves again. The
Ark would become a rustic arbour, the tree of Noah, full of
peacocks and butterflies. It's just as well. Goodness knows
what will become of the animals when they are all inside."

"What do you mean, Noah? You are going to look after
them."

"How? I have to compile an inventory of living creatures
you know; not a dictionary of words. I have to allow room
on board for the growth of populations. I am not stopping
life, but inviting it. The birds will not just sit with pall'd
appetites; they will nest under the eaves. In the nave the

jackals will couple, the mare will be covered, the she-wolf will defend her litter. The hulk must teem with life. There must be room in the dark for the mice to hide from the owl who hawks along the aisles. But there must be enough mice for the white owl to be able to feed her young, and for there to be mice when the earth is dry to receive them again."

"But you have an obligation!"

"What?"

"To separate the animals."

"Why?"

"You can't let the fox get among the roosting birds. He would bite the heads off the entire feathered kingdom. There must be bulkheads in the church, panthers this side, chamois that side."

"Do you know how to look after spiders, Cordelia?"

"No."

"Neither do I." He got up and went on to the site.

She climbed over a pile of ropes and pulleys after him. "What's that got to do with it?" He was walking fast. When she caught up with him, he had reached the paddock behind the vicarage. The horses snorted over the hedge. They went careering away. But when Noah stood by the gate, they turned and came trotting up.

"The grass is so dry," he said. "But we can look after horses; but spiders – well, I just have to let spiders be. There will be straw on board. But the lion won't eat it. The lion will eat the ox who eats the straw, unless the ox is too quick for him."

"You are actually going to risk some of the species becoming extinct?"

"But a great bundle of life will be preserved. You can call it the miraculous feeding, the magic cafeteria – where life feeds upon life, and multiplies. See how sleek and smooth his coat is. If it were rough and staring, he would be going out of condition. Noah moved his hand down the broad chine of the stallion's back. "The natural economy of the Ark doesn't bear thinking of."

They were married in January in the pouring rain. Since the church at Wormeaster was nowhere near finished, the dean invited them to the cathedral; and what began in their heads as a slight event gathered momentum. Peris Morgan would bring the choir; and then it became clear that the whole school wanted to come, for Cordelia was much loved; then it became difficult not to leave out anyone who lived in the parish. There would be the families on both sides, their own friends, and their parents' friends, and that meant the county. The advantage of a cathedral is that you can have as many people as you like. Mr Guppy groaned. He was a wine shipper, not in a very big way, and began to work out how many people would be needed to drink the profits of a year's trading in one afternoon. He booked the town hall and wondered about champagne cider which he had never touched. "Let's see," said the town clerk, opening his diary. "There will be Christmas, and the wedding, and the Epiphany fair. You realise, Mr Guppy, that with the fair in the market place, there will be a problem of getting your guests from the cathedral to the town hall." Mr. Guppy wished it might prove so.

On Holy Innocents Day, Mr Cane's Travelling Circus came from the south along the same route which Vespasian's

Second Legion must have taken from Hop Hill to Oldbury
Warren hundreds of years before. Mr Cane did not shout his
orders in Latin. He did not urge his caravans into the morning mist – '*Augusta Secunda contende!*' – but he had a fine
sense of impedimenta and pabulum, and the same expectation of an expedition for spoils. He had a dark face and sat in
the cab of the front van. It was raining steadily, so the convoy
moved more slowly than usual, and other road-users who
got caught at the back of the procession became impatient.
Someone overtook Mr Cane hooting like a psychopath. He
observed to the driver next to him, "Accidents happen when
people get angry." Fred didn't take his eyes off the road. The
wind-screen wipers weren't very efficient.

Noah packed the portable sacred things to take her
Christmas communion to old Mrs Coombes. Were it not
raining he would have gone directly across the fields and
crossed the railway line at Park Bridge. Now he would go
down the back lane to the level crossing. He stood at the
vicarage door considering the rain and the building site
before him with its gaunt, unfinished Ark. And he set off
almost nervously. He wasn't ready yet for much rain. He
wasn't ready. He wasn't even ready for his wedding. He
turned up his collar and stepped out. Half-way down the lane
he was met by a stray cow, wet and steaming. She was
marching towards the vicarage. He would tell Coombes when
he reached the farm. Noah was negotiating a large puddle
when he heard the unmistakable roar of a lion. A lion! In the
next field! He spun round. The cow was galloping towards
the Ark, the rain fell steadily. Noah waved his bag despair-
ingly, so that the sacred things rattled inside, and turned and
ran wildly down the lane to his appointment.

Just before the level crossing, sunk on its front near side, was a large van bearing the legend Cane's Travelling Circus, and the proprietor was kneeling in the road and shouting to his followers.

"The lion!" said Noah to a man bearing a jack.

"He always complains when we stop, mister."

"You mean?"

"He likes travelling, doesn't he?"

Noah, who had sprinted up to the end of the lane, stood shyly surveying the line of trucks along the main road. It was true. There was no sign of alarm. Half-way down the line was a truckload of children eating breakfast. Only the bustle of the party who changed the tyre disturbed the calm of the caravan. The lion had settled down.

The proprietor wiped his hands on his trousers, and saw Noah, with satisfaction. He inspected his hands. Noah didn't like to say that there was a dark smear in the middle of his forehead, so he cast down his eyes.

"Then we shall be off presently."

It said 9.28 on Noah's watch. "The Westering Express will be through shortly. It's usually late."

"Thank you."

He climbed up into the cab. As his face turned Noah saw that it was not a smudge but a wound, a scar, a cicatrice, in the middle of his forehead. Like a sunburst. The gypsy with the sunburst rolled the wagons and led the way over the level crossing into the rain.

It was the children's caravan that had difficulty in starting. The children waved to Noah, and the engine spluttered and they lurched off after the others. On the level crossing itself it stopped again. Noah could see the driver struggling in the

cab, trying to catch the engine again. The sequence of events
after that was confused. The lights started flashing, then the
bell, then the barrier came down and the caravan was still
stuck. The driver was out of the cab screaming to the
children. Noah stood transfixed. You could hear the express
through the driving rain. The door was open and the
children bursting out. People were running. The earth shook
with the approach of the train. Noah could see the train, and
the steps of the caravan, and the child who stood in terror at
the top. And with a great cry of despair he fled into the
caravan and took the child to him as the express struck. He
roared with pain, and the whole world was blasted and
blown wide.

He must have turned a somersault with the child, for he
landed on his feet, stood quivering, and then collapsed. The
child yelled and crawled out of his lap. The express and the
caravan were nowhere to be seen. He could taste the rain
mingled with blood running down his face. He was going to
die of shock. Blast it! He saw quite clearly the rain bouncing
on the rails, shining and falling, and he saw it all getting
smaller and smaller. He no longer wanted to breathe. Blast!
He felt so angry at the point of death. A great pain for the
life of the child swept through his body as it went numb. He
understood his salt blood as a gift, as a cordial, as at last
golden. He began to relax and to collaborate with the darkness. In fact after a day in bed, he was none the worse for
wear. And the engine-driver came to the wedding. But not
only the engine-driver. The entire company of Cane's
travelling circus stood at the back of the cathedral and when
Noah and Cordelia walked to their reception, the fairground
celebrated their arrival with the homage that no rain could

spoil, as it were king and queen. So that there were free rides for all the guests, and much good wine. And in the evening when the lights were lit on the big-wheel, Noah and Cordelia were loath to depart from all their friends in the turning, turning world.

When Shem was three and Ham was two, Japheth was born at Wormeaster vicarage, and the Dean and Chapter invited Noah to preach at Mattins on his wedding annivers- ary. He sat on the end of Cordelia's bed and read the letter. There was a fire in the grate, both because it was winter, and also because they shared the opinion that a coal fire in one's bedroom is a reminiscently luxurious thing. Ham came staggering in shrieking for justice. Cordelia interpreted it at once: "Shem has taken his book again. He's jealous. I do wish he wouldn't."

Ham's favourite book belonged to Noah. It was a display of heraldry. He lay on his stomach and turned the pages, pointing to each escutcheon in turn, and had learned like lightning to say fess, bend, pale, bordure, chevron and escarboncle. It was difficult to attend an innocent parade of erudition from such an infant without marvelling. Shem had not failed to notice his parents' special pleasure; so he regularly took his revenge.

Cordelia rested against the pillows and watched thought- fully the hostility between her older children as Noah gave the baby its bath. Then he sat content with his young- est son naked on his knee, and a warm pool formed in his lap. When Cordelia saw what had happened, the frown left her face and she laughed and held out her hands for Japheth.

"You see," said Noah agreeably, "everyone takes natural disaster more lightly than moral evil!"

He went to his study in fresh attire and wrote his Epiphany sermon. He read the five paragraphs in chapter two in St Matthew: he wrote them down as, the wise men at Jerusalem, the wise ditto at Bethlehem, the flight into Egypt, the murder of the children of Bethlehem, the return.

It's a story, all right. Is it a real story (a fairy tale or authentic)? There is simply no way of deciding *now* whether it happened or not. Neither those who would say "Well, it's in the Bible, it must be historical" nor those who would say "It's obviously a legend" have got it right.

It spoils it to think the story isn't really true. (Don't spoil it, you preacher.) But the NT isn't plain history. It is theology. Better, it is the interpretation of history by those who believe in Jesus. The evangelists are not liars. But they are makers of history rather than recorders of it. If you want to call them recorders, what they record is the theological awareness of the first groups of Jews and Gentile converts who believed, but who may not have actually seen Jesus. This story has come to them not in the newspapers, but as a sermon. It is a memorable sermon (i) because it is brilliantly done, (ii) because it is about them – about the fact that although Jesus was given to the Jewish nation, it is the Gentiles who recognised, and came and found him, and worship him. What is being faithfully recorded is the adoration of the early church.

Legend? It spoils Christianity to get all romantic about a hedge-hopping star. Whatever Christianity is about, it is not about magical gifts (gold, frankincense, myrrh) but about plain matters (daily bread, forgiveness, selfless respect for reality). I agree, the story of the wise men is incidental. But it is popular. What has to be accounted for is why Matthew has placed this story in such a prominent place, i.e. at the beginning. What has to be accounted for is the sheer fact that thousands and thousands who were never on that journey, never saw the star or the presents unpacked, have got there. It's a carol, isn't it?

I bet you don't get a Christmas card with Herod on it. But red-handed Herod is part of this Epiphany. Popular religion instinctively chooses what is happy, beautiful, comfortable, touched with a little mystery, to express the feast. It exerts a pressure on the story to make it legendary. But we can see now that the coming of the wise men is a threat to Jesus (their discovery puts him in peril; the consequences for the village are terrible).

Then Noah paused, and after a while he wrote:

> Child, who is that at the door?
> The magicians, mother.
> Streets full of circus-wheels
> Bethlehem's scholars
> Jugglers and mountebanks, lions
> And wayfaring men
> Whose chivalry has erred and strayed
> To the city of David.
>
> In carpets come the strolling Kings
> Smelling of Persia,
> A musician, a professor, and a blackamoor,
> With theatrical eyes.

E

How holy is this time of arrival!
The make-believe gypsies
Paint their wagons with treasure
And patent medicine.

Warned off by waking dreams
The unlicensed men
Fold up their pageants after dark
At the auspicious time
Slip into the confidential air,
Suffer an eclipse.
When red-handed Herod comes
In another country
They will be putting on their faces
For the next performance.

You did not intend the bogeyman
To come to life.
Consult the comedian in the looking-glass.
The eyes are stars;
Mask as chalk as the death of innocents,
And nose as blood.

What does it mean? If it is to reproduce the original it has
to be brilliant, and also about us. Noah considered the
irresponsibility of the magicians and the jealousy of the king
at the revealing of Christ. Is that it? We recognise ourselves
as playing both. Where is the situation in ordinary life where
what is true and good provokes not only admiration from us
but also antipathy? Where approval and envy go together?
Has God a place both for the homage of the old men, and

the destructive aggression of the king? Does he use both
to show us Jesus fearlessly? Why is this sermon not coming
out?

I am not taking Herod seriously. He is a murderer. What
do we know about murderers? Noah turned to the story of
Cain. As he read he decided that he would not like to defend
Cain in court.

"I will not dispute the material facts, that on such and such
a date, with a spade or other implement, Cain did batter to
death Abel his brother, and that the ground was drenched
with his blood. It is no part of the defence to offer a different
account. But observe the context of this event. It is a family
affair. Murder is very largely a family affair. (Quote Home
Office report.) So you must put from your minds any sense
of a peculiar outrage here in the murder of a brother.

"Provocation is an important element in this case. The
luck of Abel and his whole way of life represented a direct
threat to Cain. Cain was to clear the land and cultivate. But
Abel is a cowboy – and the Lord had respect to him. It means
Abel was flourishing. His over-the-hills-and-far-away life
was admired. He is as romantic as a bull-fighter. This is what
threatens the suburban life which Cain is inventing. By his
sweat Cain will recover the land to the tilth of paradise. But
Abel will swagger and trespass across all this with his beasts.
The difference becomes emphatic in their offerings to the
Lord. What has Cain got to offer? Corn and pots of marma-
lade! How shall he present a sacrifice as vivid and terrible –
and acceptable! – as the butcher Abel? This is the sacrifice
which goes to the heart of the matter. Abel is not afraid to
pour out the smoking blood and to hang the carcasses in his
shop. When the villagers see Abel sacrifice, their hair stands

on end. They say, as we all say in our hearts: Now that is to sacrifice! It is awful!

"You may have in your mind the motive of murder for profit. In this crime, in which Cain imitates his brother in the desire to have blood, nothing is gained. He sacrifices everything he has. What little civilisation he has tamed from the wild cannot be defended by such violence. Can you understand the blood of Abel contaminating Cain's ground, so that the earth itself becomes Abel, and hostile to the farmer? The valleys of corn and the pleasant park, with walls and towers, Cain's foothold, his benefice, becomes worthless to him. All of it soured, all of it spoiled. all of it cursed.

"So we approach the most significant piece of evidence in this case. It is that Cain, who is on trial for murder, is the man who speaks with the Lord. So what is the Lord's part? Is he an accomplice? We know that the Lord had provided a land full of thistles, and that Cain with his toil and technology had wished to civilise it, to promote the pattern of whatever is wholesome and a good investment, to eradicate the chaotic tanglewood. Is the Lord the source of provocation? Immediately after the slaying, the Lord says to Cain: Where is thy brother Abel? So quick! If he was so close to the event why did he not with his mighty arm ward off the spade? At least, he is present at the heart of this man's agony and desperation. You may conclude that the capacity of Cain to make havoc does not frighten the Lord as it frightens ordinary decent folk like us. Also you will notice that the Lord does not desert Cain in his wish of death; he even marks him as one who had indelibly the Lord's protection. So what is the Lord's part?

"I will suggest to you this. He does not treat Cain as

prehistoric, as emerging *homo sapiens* with homicidal violence as part of his teething troubles. So I cannot plead for Cain that you should be patient and patronise him, or ask you to remember that however many times he clubs his associates, he has a clumsy animal nature which is growing slowly into maturity, responsibility and morality. No, the Lord talks to Cain with a much deeper respect.

"He holds him responsible! What sort of defence is this? Well, the Lord takes Cain's great preoccupation with death and with that he opens for him a door into freedom. I ask this court for the same freedom. I ask you not to banish Cain to the fringes of conscious life, to the unconscious, where murder is rife and guilt not appreciated. I appeal to the Lord."

When Noah emerged from the cathedral, his family tugged him off to the Epiphany fair in the market-place. They met their old friends of the travelling circus, and the proprietor sitting on the steps of his caravan. Ham climbed over him energetically. He stood looking solemnly into that dark face. Then he pointed his finger and touched the sunburst in his forehead. "Escarboncle," said Ham.

Mr Cane bared his teeth and growled like a lion. Ham stared in his nest, and then prodded his finger against this inviting snarl and felt the sharp teeth of the gypsy. Cordelia watched, torn between politeness and anxiety. When Ham took away his finger, Mr Cane snapped his jaws. He lifted the child and went snapping and growling against the fat little stomach.

"Come along, darling," said Cordelia.

Ham looked round at his mother, then he turned back in the gypsy's arms, flung out his hands and said, "Again!"

Mr Cane considered Cordelia and laughed.

"Again!"

"Dangerous things, lions," he remarked handing back the child to his mother. Cordelia settled him in the pram opposite Japheth, and smiled nicely to the proprietor. His free gaze was disconcerting.

"Again!" repeated Ham as he was wheeled away. Cordelia bent over the pram and growled bravely. "We could walk home," she said to Noah. He was holding Shem's hand.

"The Dean is expecting us to sherry."

"Not with this rabble. I've made our excuses."

The town had the great medieval distinction of being discreet. It did not spill into its own countryside. Where the town stopped, the unlittered fields began. They could walk by the ancient way of the meadows all the way to Wormcaster.

"Winter is best," said Cordelia, breathing the fine, cold air. Pigeons rose, and filtered through the bare trees, and came to rest in clumps of ivy. The ivy shook as if it were full of squirrels. The birds were feeding on berries. "They want to build a road through here. A relief road! And a huge carpark. We don't need a flood really, do we? People will do it for you."

"That's different."

"What is the flood, then? It is an expression for the ominous, or that we're heading for catastrophe. It is the volume of humanity. That Mr Cane, he doesn't like crowds really."

"He depends on them for his livelihood!"

"But he is a private man, a secret man. He is contemptuous

of the pooling of the knowledge of society, the sharing of social justice. What he does is to turn up with something unusual, and make everything else look secondhand."

They lifted the pram over a stile. Noah began carrying Shem on his shoulders.

"I had rather felt that the flood would be like the onset of insanity," he said. "While the church is being built, I can come and go on the dry ground. I can go into the Ark, and it is safe to come out again. But when the water comes, I shall have to sail on that tide; and I will not be my own master. I shall not be able to come back."

"You mean withdrawing from the dry ground where we all live?"

"I used to be anxious every time it rained," he said. "But the flood may be more sinister. I would take my chance against water, I suppose. But what if the flood is nothing? How would one detect the rising level of nothing? It would be peculiar, wouldn't it, to be engulfed by nothing? Could the Ark float in that? It wasn't built for it. This nothing is more alien than water; it has a hostility which the sea never had." They went on in silence. The sky became as brown as brass.

"The invisible deluge!"

"I wouldn't like it to wash my brains."

"What you have got is a case of the evil imaginations. Didn't they like your sermon, or something?"

The children began to bicker with the cold.

"Soon be home; soon be home! Cold weather is nice, don't you understand?" said Cordelia. She worried Noah. He stopped the pram, put down his burden, and just

before Wormeaster came into view, he clutched Cordelia
by her marvellous hair. It was the anniversary of their
wedding.

She put her arms round him.

"What is it?"

"Snow coming!" he said, comforting himself in the
friendly smell of her hair.

When it snowed, Cordelia moved into the study and read
Noah's books after the children's bedtime. It was the
warmest room in the vicarage.

"All the Inlets, Under-Seas, Lakes, etc. made Fountains . . .
Spouts of Vapours to darken the Sky, and vast Spouts
of Water rising like Fountains, making a dreadful Noise,
rising in the Sea, and running to the Sea, and the Sea
rising and driving the People to the Mountain Tops,
their last shift; where they with Fright, Rain, Hunger
or those who survived till the Waters came, perished by
them."

"Who is it? Hutchinson?"

"*Moses's Principia* 1749 – listen! No Distinction now of
Dry-Land and Sea; everything lay in the Channel of one
River. No Springs or Lakes, no pleasant Fountains; but all
things were swallowed up of the huge Waves. No Plants,
Flowers, or Trees; no Cities, no Plains, no Mountain Tops,
but all Things had suffered Shipwrack and were buried in
one common Sepulchre."

Noah looked up from his desk. "It is just as well."
He folded his arms, and rested on the desk, with his eyes
closed.

"What do you mean?"

He looked at Cordelia without really seeing her. He propped his head in his hands.

"Remember the Diocesan inspectors?"

"Those nervous little fellows who were here last week?"

"They were the Diocesan inspectors."

"What about them?"

"Oh, it's nothing. You see, I wanted them to come and tremble with admiration. Do you know what I wanted? I wanted them to come and put a hand on the holy wood of the Ark, and kneel down! I wanted their astonishment and their recognition of the grand design of the mystical Ark. I expected them not only to get out their official stamp, but also the certificates of their own devotion. They should have issued me the bills of lading for live cargo! And that I wanted, the humility, which acknowledges that the voyage is not for them, but that it is everyone's salvation. I wanted them to receive their own doom in the achievement of the Ark with the same dignity that Eli received the bad tidings from Samuel. That's what I wanted, their horror and their pride that the Ark which has been preparing is now ready."

Cordelia looked sympathetically at her husband. "They were very quiet over tea. Just not awfully intelligent, that's what I thought."

"They've turned it down."

"Oh lovey!"

He read it out aloud. "My board has therefore regretfully concluded that the proposed structure does not meet minimum diocesan standards, and advise that it should be classified unfit for worship."

"Oh, Noah, that's mean!"

He shook his head sadly.

"Very sensible decision. If there is no Ark, how can there be a Flood? But if the Ark is attempted, it serves as a warning. The credible threat of a Flood would be sufficient, perhaps, to cure complacency. Here's a man trying to tell us that doom is upon us. His doom-machine is in fact impracticable – it's knocked up out of orange-boxes – but he shows us the seriousness of our position. It might work."

She picked up the letter. "Unfit for worship! What do they mean? They have no idea. How could they judge the Ark? It is unique! How awful! What did they say, as a matter of fact, when you went round?"

Noah stepped to the window, pushed the curtains aside. The moon was out and Wormeaster Church looked black and queer in the snow.

"It's formidable, thank God."

"It's wonderful," said Cordelia by his side.

"The architect thought he detected Viking influence. They all thought it was too bloody dark inside!"

"Peris Morgan says it's numinous."

"You see," said Noah, "they are not coming! Not even Peris Morgan. That is the problem. I know they think the Ark is a little family joke. But what will happen? What did Hutchinson say? It is not to be borne, the panic of that extermination of all those we have known, the hopeless running uphill, the last clambering over flesh and fighting for air. It is just another case of the cattle trucks emptying into the gas chambers. So tell me! What master-mind contemplates that as a solution? It is outrageous! He who intends a flood, will he come down afterwards as well, and rummage through the corpses, and make a pile of all the children's shoes?"

"Noah!"

"Face it! Who could conspire such genocide? It is a wonderful indictment against an immoral purpose that this building has been officially condemned by the church."

"But you love the Ark!"

"It is a terrible vocation, like death."

"What will you do?"

"We have a delay of execution, don't we?"

It lasted ten years, and then another ten, and Noah and his sons steadily improved the building, secured some recognition from the diocese, and the last wish of the headmaster to lie there, before his funeral, was granted. Visitors came to admire the carving that Ham did, the bench-ends with sunbursts. One especially, a smart girl with dark curls, who giggled at him round the immense wood pillars, disturbed the carver. Her name was Jemima and he took her home to the vicarage. She saw Shem, and blushed because he was so handsome. They were married in the church on a May morning, and Ham picked angrily on a sweet child of the village called Keren-Happuch. Japheth wooed a solemn girl whose name was Kezia. And that winter Noah was laid up with rheumatism.

Cordelia picked the leaves off the grave of Peris Morgan. The vicarage was quiet since the boys had left home. She walked into the gloomy church, smelt the acacia wood and climbed to the organ loft. *Beatus vir!* she played, *Beatus vir!* and the tears ran down her face. What was the matter? They were all coming home at Christmas, and Noah is getting better, and Peris Morgan is safe from the wrath to come. Cordelia!

The family played Christmas games, and were preparing for bed when the firmament was opened. Noah was trying to ring up the archdeacon about the services for Holy Innocents in the morning, but he couldn't get through. The door bell was jangling away, and when he opened the door, the dark gale filled the house. Out of the pouring rain came the gypsy proprietor. He took off his humble hat, and nodded continuously. Noah stood before him in silence. Mr Cane was soaked to the skin. His face gleamed. Cordelia came down the stairs and saw Noah raise his hands towards the huddled visitor, and drop them in a gesture of despair. He heard her footfall, and without shifting his gaze, he said to his wife behind him: "Cordelia, tell the children to get dressed again."

Mr Cane turned a bright eye upon Noah. "The telegraph poles are down."

"The animals?"

"The animals have been released."

"I am ashamed." Noah bowed his head.

"Do not be ashamed," he said kindly. "If God is gracious, why should his work tonight be known as vicious? If he overwhelms his creation, does this not speak of his colossal passion and pouring out of himself in love? The turbulence of such great love, and the courage which risks all hope of survival upon one family, is the sort of risk I understand God would take."

He took Noah's hand, and led him to the vicarage door. "It is raining hard; and it is time to go. As for me, who knows if it is not a great blessing to drown? You are afraid now, because you think it is the worst thing that could happen. But we are marked indelibly with the Lord's protection. If I go to die and you to live, who knows whose luck is the better?"

The family went through the howling rain into the church. And when the doors were sealed, it slipped its site and floated from Wormeaster.

IV

THE GREAT DEEP

Noah sat by himself on deck in the grey air. The flood-water was flat, not like sea-water, like pond-water. It stretched away a dull metal into the murk. In a big area of indistinctness lay the Ark. There was nothing else in the universe to focus on. The lack of real things was bad for the eyes. This one cell, this fragile crucible, this ganglion was the one place of imperfection in an abstract current of emptiness. *Tohu wa bohu!* It threatened his soul and turned his stomach. To sit here was to challenge the abyss. Noah looked furtively up into the wet air. It was lighter; but he could not tell if the light was failing or increasing. He closed his eyes so that the flood would not blind him. He wished to assure himself of the support of the Ark beneath him. I made it, and therefore I am on it.

In self-defence he tried to make his mind work. How many sails are there on a fully rigged ship? Describe and discuss the plants in a herbaceous border in order of height. Write notes on any of the following: anchusa, acanthus, agapanthus. Is a class a member of itself, or not? But his bunk-hole was none of these things. He could not withdraw from his terror of the flood into these matters of interest, but only increase his giddiness, until he began theologising. And there he calmly recognised that he was divided between two thoughts.

There is and can be no God, he thought, in such a void; for nothing broods over these waters except the hulk and its builder. This consideration hung stationary with Noah. It was a simple truth, and came to him with a reassuring sense of resignation. If the Ark had at that moment then opened her timbers to let in the quiet sea, if she had slowly settled and then gone down with all hands, Noah would have yielded. The air would not have rung with a final emergency. There would be no clinging to spars, raft-building, ducking for the children, loosing horses in the dark stables under the water-line. The lethargy of the flood would cover them. Noah did not construct this thought. It was simply apparent, and remained to balance whatever else he was thinking.

It was a positive assistance to his other thought which was an honest awareness of God's presence. God haunts us, he thought. There is nowhere else for him to be. Therefore he is with us. The ghosts and the spirits of the air have nowhere in the whole earth to rest the soles of their feet except on this undoubted deck. Anyone who has seen the flood would recognise that only here could God rest, with Noah. It is the only place where there is any shape or definition. Noah understood it; he felt it. That is why the form of his meditation was like a conversation resumed after the company had fallen silent.

"I am forgetting your walking on the water," said Noah to himself.

"It is a miracle."

"Yes, it is a miracle. I continually forget it."

"Aren't miracles to be forgotten? Aren't there more important things?"

"I should have remembered it, sir," said Noah.

"It was there all the time."

"Yes, it was there all along. It is like a man who married a woman with a sweet smile and an enormous nose. The nose is there all the time, but he never notices. Except sometimes he surprises himself by seeing what he has been looking at and says: How could I marry a woman of such remarkable ugliness?"

"You are inviting me to say that my walking on the water is an embarrassment to you."

"Oh, no. It is a comfort to me, sir, to remember your walking on the water just now. For all that it is a wild miracle, I am drawn to it. I think I have always preferred your wild miracles to your respectable ones."

"What is a respectable miracle?"

Noah didn't answer. Then he said: "I'm talking to myself, aren't I?"

"If you think that, how can we continue?"

"A respectable miracle," said Noah, "is one you can understand, if you like, edifying – like all the cures, the works of mercy among the sick."

"What is a wild miracle?"

"Well, this one we have in mind, walking on the water – and the one about the pigs, for instance."

"Which pigs?"

Noah smiled to himself. "The ones that went rushing down-hill."

"Now that is not a miracle about pigs, is it, Noah?"

"No, it's not. It's about you and the man Legion." As he spoke, Noah saw it, Jesus and the demoniac in the odd light, sitting next to each other in a landscape of steep places. Every ikon shares that sharp light. Had it been raining? The pair who exchanged looks of such serenity were perched on an idiotic terrain, with thunder in the air, and far away down the mountain sheer the pigs were falling in a frenzy to the sea. The precipices and the electric wind were in motion. Only the seated figures were like stone kings.

"It is misleading to call that the story of the Gadarene swine. The two calm men are not obscured by the running of the pigs. That is a detail in the background. (It is like Bellini's picture of the Resurrection. In the background there is a rabbit eating a lettuce.) Each of the two is sitting, clothed, and in his right mind. Ikons share such rationality, the reasonableness of the wild man who has washed his face, combed his hair, and come to his senses. But how is it conveyed – in gold and Byzantine – the wreckage of Legion? With what pallor is indicated the majesty of madness spent, and the healing of the batty giant? In these same faces how is it conveyed – a look of such sanity found that could never be lost again, such wit, such health, such innocence of eye, such wearing of peace like a diadem?"

Noah remarked upon the love of these two identical twins who took their ease together upon a demented hill. He said: "How could anyone tell as they sit shoulder to shoulder, or in the look of recognition between them, which one is the Christ? You are not different from that Legion, are you, sir? You are not different from me."

"But I am different. My walking on the water reminded you of that."

"It is unconventional," Noah admitted.

"You said you were drawn by the wild miracles. Is it just that you are pleased that I am able to disturb your scientific friends by being unconventional?"

F

"I expect you love scientifically respectable people with the same passion that cured the demoniac."

"We have reached a point of curiosity, like a nose of unusual proportions. What will you do next?"

"If I were at home, I should begin to compare the texts, and the commentaries upon the miracle."

"But you have left that equipment behind you."

"I could have said that," Noah reflected. "In fact, I am composing your replies." He looked out at the vacant water. "At least I would be on the same side as the evangelists when it comes to miracles. They are all four of them up to the ears in mythology. They live in a world which believes quite literally in demons, and demons which ravenously await permission to enter pigs, so that they can taste the excitement of violent death. But it goes against the grain of the evangelists to recount miracles in order to make supernatural fireworks. If it were the intention of any of them to recount a miracle as a magic event interrupting the natural course of things, as a marvel soliciting faith, then I should have to say that the lesson of the temptations of Jesus was being ignored. The temptation to jump off the pinnacle of a temple, however impressive a display it would have been, was to be resisted. But that lesson was noted and understood by the evangelists. Consequently, if a miracle in their accounts reads like magical intervention inviting me to adore, then I'm inclined to say it can't be their fault. But, since they are not in the least shy of miracles, even of the ones which appear to have precisely this discreditable aspect, my view is that they are handling awkward material faithfully."

"Do you believe in miracles, Noah?"

"That is a trap. It expects me to reply with a general

statement. But I am wary of generalisations. If we set out to discuss the question of miracles, we should go astray at once. Each miracle is its own question."

"Don't you think they might all join up somewhere?"

"Well, I prefer to think that each miracle is inexplicable in its own way."

"Very well. But people like coherence."

"Yes, and it leads them to say things like – miracles can't happen."

"And – everything is a miracle?"

"Both these are general statements," Noah explained swiftly. "But they abuse ordinary language; the first, in suggesting that the word 'miracle' has no reference, the second, in giving the word such a width of reference that it can no longer have any distinct use at all."

"All right, Noah; suppose what you say is true. Suppose the gospel writers hoarded my miracles carefully, did not blunder, are to be trusted. Suppose also that it is a mistake to come at a miracle with a theory about miracles. What would you discover by comparing the accounts of my walking on the water?"

"As I recall," said Noah, "they each tell it differently. But I am speaking without the book, and all the time I am terrified by the flood. How can we continue? You are only here because there is nowhere else to be, is there?"

Noah felt himself losing the struggle to make sense. "In Mark it was a sermon. I suppose it was about confidence," he said weakly. "I don't remember."

"And when even was come, the ship was in the midst of the sea, and he alone on the land. And he saw them toiling in rowing; for the wind was contrary unto them: and about the fourth watch of the night he cometh unto them, walking upon the sea, and would have passed by them. But when they saw him walking upon the sea, they supposed it had been a spirit, and cried out: for they all saw him, and were troubled. And immediately he talked with them, and saith unto them, Be of good cheer: it is I; be not afraid. And he went up unto them into the ship."

Noah listened in such wonder that he did not hear Cordelia climb on deck. She looked into Noah's worn face.

"What is it, lovey? You are crying."

"It's nothing. It's the Bible."

"Are you hungry?"

Noah looked at his wife. "Would you say we are moving? Do you have the feeling that we are slipping down-hill?"

Cordelia studied the flat ocean, and the empty sky. "I thought there would be storms," she said.

"It has been like this for days."

"Do you mean we are actually going down a slope of water?" Cordelia stretched out her feet in front of her as she sat, and tried to picture the deck tilting, and the whole Ark sliding down-hill.

"But just imagine," said Noah, "if someone had pulled the plug out, and the water was going down at an immense rate, you wouldn't notice it, would you, until you got into the mill-race?"

The idleness of the flood and the Ark were plain to Cordelia. There was no change, no objects going past to show them where they were, or in which direction they were going. There was nothing for them to be relative to. "There is no encouragement to imagine momentum or direction," she replied. "It's all a matter of balance."

"We are near to God," said Noah.

"What d'you mean?"

"Do you feel apprehensive?"

"No, well, you make me feel apprehensive. You have been sitting here too long."

It is a creepy place. It is featureless, and silent. It ought to be utterly boring. But it isn't."

"I don't understand."

"Prayer should be boring," said Noah to her.

"Who said anything about prayer?"

"I'm telling you."

"You've been too long up here. You have been infected by the stillness of the deep water, that's all. You warned us yourself. You told us to keep our attention upon the things in the Ark, didn't you? Come on, Noah. Let's go down. I don't like it up here."

He laughed. "It's all right. Do you know that lots of people have strained to reach a state which is called contemplation? We have been given it on a plate. First steps for contemplatives include the steady obliteration of everything round them, before they can enter the interior silence and vacancy. We, however, have simply sailed in. It is remarkable."

"Noah, please."

"There is the flood, of course. But no one could relate to that. That is why it is the flood."

"You are lonely and hungry," said Cordelia. "And anyway, it's getting dark."

He leant back. It was true; the light was failing. He waited, and then said softly: 'Listen!' Cordelia listened. All the sound that there was then in the universe flowed from under the hatches of the Ark. The roosting birds sang their incongruous agricultural songs in that waste of water and dark air, such calling and whistling, such natural melody, such instinctive competitions, such a chorus, that Noah sniffed nature again, and went down cheerfully into the ship.

"I wish to explain," said Noah, at the supper table, "the difference between the separate accounts of the miracle of the walking on the water!"

"I would rather play Fingers In," said Shem hopefully. Noah looked round his family and the beautiful girls.

"The table's too big." It was the great kitchen table which they had had at home, scrubbed and reliably familiar.

"We can manage," they all agreed.

Cordelia looked at him.

"All right. Fingers In."

The youngest came and sat next to him, immediately.

"I quite like it in the Ark," she said pulling in her chair. "You won't look at my cards, will you?"

Noah yawned. "Why should I?"

"Or you could play, and I'll just watch."

She was Ham's wife, and she was yet a child. She looked at you when she spoke. Her name was Keren-happuch, but she was known as Poo or Happoo, a friendly person. She worked tirelessly and loved the animals. She considered herself dim.

"What are we playing for?"

"To see who is the winner."

"I know," said Ham, "let's make it exciting. Let's play for forfeits."

Poo enquired if the loser paid the forfeit.

"Yes."

"I'm bound to lose. What will the forfeit be?"

He paused in the middle of the shuffle. "You'll see. We'll make them up, when the time comes."

"I don't mind."

The Markan account of the walking on the water, thought Noah, as he considered his first card, is admirable both in its economy, and in its discernment that Jesus immediately talked with them at the height of the miracle and in their plain distress. Was this a paradigm of the divine conversation, both that it is miraculous and known at the extremities of human trouble? Is not Job the case where anguish and depressive illness become the auditorium for the voice of God? Noah's card was an ace. But he did not bet on it, and was proved correct.

Two cards were dealt. They rapped the table in unison. Four fingers were put in.

"Ah; four bids for two tricks!"

Noah's fist and Poo's small hand lay side by side. Her forefinger was sticking out. He had not bid. She looked up sideways and made her eyes bulge. "You're safe," she said pleasantly.

She won both tricks, and a mixture of delight and disgust went round the table. It was Noah's deal.

Three cards; if we are to say that it is a sermon by St Mark about confidence, then what is the ground of this confidence for the men toiling in the boat? It is that this Jesus who comes to them walking on the water is indeed the Messiah. They are Old Testament men, and they witness the expectation of the Old Testament coming true. For the Old Testament expects God to be able to subdue the sea, to walk over chaos, and to rescue us all from the great deep, literally from the storms of the sea as well as from the sombreness and the sudden fury of evil. Thou art the God that doeth wonders. It is messianic longing. The sailors knew the psalms.

> The waters saw thee, O God, the waters saw thee, and were afraid: the depths also were troubled. The clouds poured out water, the air thundered: and thine arrows went abroad. The voice of thy thunder was heard round about: the lightnings shone upon the ground; the earth was moved, and shook withal. Thy way is in the sea, and thy paths in the great waters: and thy footsteps are not known.

Noah played his hand mechanically. The miracle is in the poetry, and in the confidence which is conveyed by St Mark's sermon.

"It's your turn."

"Oh, is it? Oh, yes."

"Hurry up. You're spoiling it."

Noah lost, and began to concentrate on the game.

Tomorrow he would see how Matthew put it differently. It would be a characteristic difference. He didn't like it when other people didn't attend to their play, so he stared resolutely at his next hand. Poo was doing quite well. Japheth was silent and losing.

Cordelia was amused. Kezia was flushed and nervous. Shem was boisterous. Poo was hopping in her seat. Ham was bold and bid extravagantly which made everyone laugh.

"Hooray," said Jemima loudly, throwing away her last card.

"Who's won?"

"Who's lost, you mean?"

Poo was grinning. "Not me!"

"I have," said Japheth.

"Forfeit!"

"All right, silly. What's the forfeit?"

"Not to lose your temper."

"Or call people names."

"The forfeit," announced Ham, "is to go down to the hold, and bring back some eggs . . . alone." For the first time that evening the eight passengers on the Ark fell silent. They were short of food. It was an obvious solution to go down into the hold and steal eggs. It was dangerous to go down there.

"It's not fair."

"I don't mind."

"You daren't."

"What d'you mean I daren't?" Japheth stood up.

"Noah, you are not to permit it."

He looked at his wife. Then he looked at his sons. To enter the dark hold full of animals and to emerge safely with ducks' eggs or gulls' eggs, required both nerve and wit. The wild beasts were loose in the dark. It had never been in Noah's plans to separate them.

Besides being a learned and agreeable man, Noah's father had been an accomplished poacher, a sober, industrious and respected man, friend both of the clergy and of the police, never suspected, in his whole life never once caught trespassing in pursuit of game. He was an eccentric and an amateur who kept his counsel. He knew the ways of the professionals, and could judge exactly where they had laid

their wires, set snares or hidden their nets; but he never re-
vealed himself to them, nor disturbed their trade. The poaching gangs were their own worst enemies. They made too
much noise; their conspiracy was almost certain to include
talkative fellows; they were obliged to sell the bag to rascals.
He himself was solitary, and poached only for his own table.
He sympathised with the recklessness of the poachers, especially when the wages of the country labourer were low
and gamekeepers abundant; their cruelty he disliked. True
skill and secrecy were his ambition; to train a dog, and to
anticipate game, were a gentleman's recreation. The out-
witting of the keepers and the provision of good fresh food
were a bonus. He liked free things. To collect blackberries
and sloes he considered a moral duty; and to eat stolen
pheasant was a blessing.

He was already no longer so fleet of foot when he began
to instruct his son. From him Noah learned how to hide and
how to judge the weather, when to take the gun, and when
to leave it at home. In severe weather, when the hares are
stupid, he showed him how to take these creatures by hand,
catching them behind the poll. He taught him how to persuade the game that it has not been seen. He knew the art of
taking roosting birds in a loop of horsehair. He could catch
hedge-birds by whistling, and practised Noah in imitating
the notes of finches. He could stand under a tree and fill it
with wood-pigeons. Noah learned the trick of cupping his
hands and calling the birds to pitch in. The technique of the
long net and the gate net set up in silence in the dark was
passed from father to son. Noah was used to seeing salmon,
rabbit and partridge on the dining-room table. Now he
learned how to watch and to intercept the game in the cold

night. He discovered the pros and cons of poaching when the wind was blowing and the oaks roaring. His father's wonderful stealth and balance as they slipped through a covert was an example to him. The stillness of the hunter and the hunted excited him. He had seen his father raise his finger to the dog Jessie, so that she held her own tail still when it had been wagging and beating against the bracken. They had all held this poise and watched the gamekeeper tramp by glaring and not seeing, and they could hear him winding his watch. It was important to sit as close as hares, explained his father.

"I'm getting too old to run."

Thus when Noah had learned to which wood to go for nuts, where the mushrooms were to be gathered, how to work with ferrets, where to find plovers' eggs, how to bait pheasant runs, and how to stand so quiet that a mole will burrow right up to your feet and lift your shoe, when he was well acquainted with the natural history of foxes, kestrels, herons, hedgehogs, when he had tamed jackdaws, taken tench from ponds and trout from streams, when he had cured an owl of pneumonia, caught vipers, and learnt to ride, his father began to stay in at night and sleep in his warm bed.

Noah too had never been caught "in possession of a coney" as they say in court. Now he in turn looked at his sons, and tidied up the pack of cards.

V

THE DARK CHURCH

"There is no problem!" said Japheth. Ham felt intact. It was a familiar situation of obstinacy which the family would register in a moment. He waited judiciously. Happoo was glaring at him.

"Part of the problem," she said, "is that you two should recognise that there is one."

"Don't let's have any forfeits," said Cordelia looking straight at Noah. "It's a silly, dangerous, and useless suggestion." Why didn't he support her?

"But we are all hungry!" said Ham.

"Well, I'll make you some coffee. At least there's plenty of water." Cordelia was very conscious of their hunger. The supper had been frugal, like all the meals of late. They had grossly underestimated how long the flood would last. What had impressed her was the way they all behaved so well. They sat at meal times as cheerfully as if their tiny rations had been a banquet. She had watched Noah politely cutting the rind off his little piece of cheese; and then, later on, reaching out to his plate, fingering the rind, and then secretly gobbling it up. What was he hesitating for now?

"It's bedtime, isn't it?" said Noah gently.

So that was it! He was going to wait until they were all asleep and then go and do what Japheth had been dared to do.

He had decided that he was the only person capable of bird-nesting in the Ark.

"We want to decide it now," said Shem.

"We can decide in the morning."

Japheth stood up. "There's nothing to decide!"

Noah slapped the cards down on the table. "Sit down!"
It was being hungry. It made them all irritable.

Cordelia heated the water and made the coffee stronger than the ration.

"Nobody knows if there are any eggs there, anyway," said Jemima. "What lovely coffee!" Cordelia handed Noah his mug. He agreed. She could see that he knew. If anyone knew where the eggs were, it would be Noah. He knew every inch of that church. He had designed it. He could walk about the rafters with his eyes closed. It was dangerous; but the frightening thing was that her husband was the one man qualified to go. He was spare. He had already produced his family. He would also do the most professional job, un-flustered by rivalry.

"It's filthy down there. I'm not going," said Kezia.

"No one's asking you, dear. The subject is closed."

"A black church!" said Ham. "Full of delicious eggs; it's a man's job, all right."

"Oh, shut up, will you?"

"Don't you see?" he replied. "It is a simple matter of elimination. None of the womenfolk should be invited to go. And Noah, with respect, should be disqualified for reasons of age. That leaves three of us."

"You and Japheth are disqualified," said Happoo quickly, "because you are both trying to turn this into a contest."

Jemima patted Shem's arm. "That leaves you, darling."

"I didn't mean that," said Happoo. "I'm sorry."

Noah intervened. "It just shows that this is not necessarily the best method for deciding things."

"What is?"

"If we are agreed that it would be sensible for one man to go foraging for eggs in the Ark, then the one who goes must have both the authority and the opportunity."

"Do you mean the authority of the rest of us?"

"There are different sorts of authority," said Noah. "Some are better than others. There is, for example, the authority of coercion. If Japheth had a gun, he could simply make us agree not to interfere with his intention to go to the door and set off on this escapade. It is not a very good authority."

"But impressive."

"All right. But lawless; you see, rules have a better authority."

"There are no rules about bird-nesting."

"But there are rules, of a sort, within a family. You have already expressed an unwritten rule that we don't ask the women to do dangerous jobs."

"You are going to tell us," said Japheth, "that the father has a certain authority in the family."

"I won't press it," he said. "In fact parental authority is something which diminishes with time."

"It is replaced by honour," said Jemima.

"While it lasts, it is like the authority of the expert. Now that is a notable authority."

"Those who know better than we do."

"In matters of doubt," said Noah, "one usually takes the advice of the expert, whose office and authority it is to answer."

"In this case, we need an expert poacher," suggested Happoo.

"You can disagree with the experts," insisted Japheth.

"On what authority?"

"Your own!" he said.

"That's silly!"

"No, it is undeniable," said Noah. "Japheth is right, and it is a very high authority – to say, when you have heard the experts, that you see it differently."

Japheth realised that his chance was slipping from him. Noah was not only insinuating his authority as head of the family. He was claiming expertise too, the one who understood animals, the one who knew his way about the church better than any of them. Why did he want to interfere?

"Suppose I say that I know best in this matter, and that I should go?" There was resentment in his voice.

"There is a higher authority than that," answered Noah.

"Whose?"

"The authority of God. If God had commanded someone to provide food for all on board, that person would have the highest authority to go . . ." His voice was drowned in a great roar which echoed through the ship and up into the bellringers' chamber where they were sitting.

"Wow!" said Happoo, putting her hand in her mouth.

"Keep still!" said Noah. He rose quietly to his feet. It came again. It was one carnivrous roar, a dangerous, angry, open-toothed sound. Noah tiptoed across the chamber. There was a large laundry basket in the corner. He fished inside and brought out a small shopping basket, emptied the pulleys, clothes-pegs and oddments out of it, and by unfastening his belt and threading through the handle, slung it at his waist.

"You see," he regarded his family, "it's the opportunity that really counts."

"What d'you mean?"

"The one who goes is the one who has the opportunity. The lion has killed. That means there is just a moment's truce below." He stood by the newel stairs, brushing the dust off his cassock.

"Noah!"

"I claim to go, because I recognise the opportunity. It's quite safe. All the beasts of prey will be occupied waiting for their turn at the carcass, and a man can pass unnoticed through the jungle!"

"Noah!"

"Won't be long. Shem; come down after me. When I'm out you are to lock the door. Understood?"

Shem followed him down the bellringers' stairs. It grew darker at every winding turn, and stuffier. They were descending into the bowels of the ship. The idea of filling the church with animals had appealed to him once as lively and picturesque. But the reality was miserable. It was like a warehouse infested with rats. At the bottom he saw Noah shifting the bolts of the door in the dim light. His father turned and put a finger to his lips, and Shem regarded him with awe. Noah grinned and patted the basket like a man going shopping for his wife. He pointed to the door, took a deep breath, and nodded. Shem, as reluctant as a prison warder sending a man to the dungeons, hesitated. Noah sighed, took another breath, and conveyed his willingness to start. Shem opened the door into the darkness, and Noah was gone instantly.

The amazing air smacked into Shem's face. It scalded his nose. It rushed so darkly heavy and hircine into his throat, that tears came, and the skin of his head wrinkled and rippled, and crackled in his ears. He leant upon the door instinctively to bottle up the crowded smell of animals; and had to school himself not to slam the bolts in disgust. He slid them home silently, and shaking all over, he climbed fast into the crystal atmosphere above.

"Did he say, by any chance, how he was getting back?"

"Are you feeling all right, Shem?"

"He was very bossy and pompous about going, wasn't he?"

"Have some coffee, dear."

"This is like the air-raid shelters, isn't it?"

Shem did not say anything. He sat white and serious at the table. In the lamplight Kezia spread out the cards for a game of patience.

Noah stood in the black nave without stirring a muscle. He waited until he could breathe. The hot air which was louder than any sound affrighted his lungs with its rancour. Then he went on waiting until he could hear above the clamour of his own blood warning him to retreat. If the door were not locked behind him, he would have wriggled home to the bellringers' chamber like a salmon up a weir. He pleaded with himself to settle the question of the wind; and decided he was down-wind. But the air was too thickly confused with scents. He had not moved. The door was still behind him. But his prowess to find direction dissolved in such an appalling darkness. It was grievous. It was too close, and the hair on his body kept rejecting the animal ferocity of it. He stood in a cloud of his own automatic nervous reflexes, and ground his teeth for shame. Inside him there was a wailing that wanted to rise to his gorge and be uttered so that he would be given away in this outer darkness. Allow me to stop shrieking, he prayed. Be still!

He put out his hands before him and tested the darkness. He turned his head and considered the oppressive silence. He moved his weight, and felt through his shoe at the slack litter on the wooden floor. He withdrew his foot again and waited. Then he heard at last what he needed. It was a sudden snarling and commotion, a dispute over the prey. And it came from the north transept! It was like someone turning the light on. Game were instantly drifted up in his direction. He knew where he was! With the back of his hand he touched the flank of one of the deer family and felt it shiver. He was, after all, standing in his own church. He had assumed that the kill would have been right in the middle of the nave, and that the rest of the menagerie would have scattered from that point and taken cover along the walls of the church. Now, as long as he went up the south aisle, he would be safe. He would have to count the pillars. He stroked the gentle, admirable beast whose home was this darkness, and sidled past.

The journey was longer than he thought. Each time he found the safety of a pillar, he had to wait. His knees were trembling with exertion because the floor was so treacherously slimy. His horses had dragged these tree trunks down from the jocund woods of Wormeaster Sleight. He reached the sixth pillar and felt with extreme caution for the front pew. His fingers came to rest on a small, hard object. It was a hymn-book. Before him now was a blind space. It was the crossing. On his right was the south transept; on his left was the sound of someone eating celery. Almost directly in front of him would be the pulpit. Between him and the pulpit he expected to meet the opposition. He put down the hymn

book and took his chance. He stepped straight forward. At
the third step he stopped and reached out with his left hand.
It was the carving on the pulpit! He turned left, and found
fingerholds in the carved wood. He was ready to flee, but he
stood and wiped his shoes silently one by one against the
skirt of his cassock. The picture of the climb was clear to him.
It was reasonable to suppose that the pulpit would be occupied, so he would go up on the outside, and thence to the
screen. All the most accessible ledges, he judged, would be
some creature's home. That is why he had chosen the most
difficult route up to the tie-beams. He braced himself against
the pulpit. The wood creaked. The chewing noise stopped
abruptly, and Noah scented trouble. In one moment his feet
were kicking and scraping against the wood, and the next he
was scrambling, flying, swinging up into the roof like a small
primate and running along the boughs through the forest of
rafters in the starless night.

He sat down in high excitement, straddling one of the
principal trusses, and opened his cassock. His shirt was soaked
with sweat. He turned back his cuffs so that his hands were
free to poach, and shook with laughter without uttering a
sound. What great comfort to sleep here in the warm eaves!
How safe it was in the rigging high above the cargo! Oh,
Grinling Gibbons, you could not have carved a better ascent
into the roof-tree of my Ark!

It seemed to Noah that the darkness was not so thick
where he sat. It was as if the climate of the flood outside were
brighter than the pitch black of the nave, and penetrated the
roof-shingles. He pulled the basket round to the front, and
wormed along the eaves, working the south pitch. It was
child's play. Without even disturbing the sitting birds, he

could charm the warm eggs from under them. Though he selected only one from each clutch, the basket filled rapidly. Confidence had completely returned to him. He would make the traverse to the north side of the building by the tie-beam over the chancel step.

He worked his way across the beam on hands and knees, and when he met the rafters of the north slope, he stood and balanced in the dark. He felt again into the eaves. His hand was among fluffy things. Pheasant chicks! He pulled it back as if he had been stung, and began at once to retreat along the beam as fast as he could. But he was too slow! He cowered from the attack, and flung up an arm to protect his face; but the hen pheasant came out like a thunderbolt, flying at him with every feather in her body. Silly bird! He spun from her, and was losing his foothold on the thin beam. He reached out deliberately for the kingpost, missed it, trod upon air, and plunged backwards, flailing his arms, and hit the beam where he couldn't catch hold of it, bounced off, and fell wildly into the black choir of the Ark's hold.

The brothers sprang to their feet round the table.

"He's done for!" Ham spoke while the echo of the crash still reverberated.

"I'm going," began Japheth.

"It was all my idea!" said Ham fiercely.

Shem barred the way. "We don't know what has happened!"

"He has fallen," said Cordelia in a voice of stone.

"We don't know whether he is alive or dead," said Shem. Poo protested. "At least we must open the door!"

"Let me go," said Japheth.

"You stay here! I am the oldest!" Shem descended again

until he reached the door. The bad air had no terror for him now. He hurled the door wide, and strained to hear in the darkness. The church was silent. The darkness stood like a wall before his face. "Noah," he whispered. There was nothing. "Noah?" He said it louder. Then he filled his lungs with the stoat-laden wind, and cried: "No-aah!" with all his might.

"Noah!" It was his name. His name was being called at a vast distance. It was a comforting sound. It was a blessing. In the nursery thus his name had been called to him after he had suffered nightmares. It had recovered him. Noah breathed quietly and composed himself to sleep again. He was lying in the warm sun, on the sea-turf, and his smile was full of his holiday.

"Noah!" He blinked into the darkness. He had fallen; it was all right. Someone had fallen. It was nothing. He was going on holiday, slipping into the sea. He was free to go without the least feeling of regret. Oh, yes; he had fallen! That was it. He was crumpled, but in his nakedness at last, he knew himself, and could be still. "Noah!" It was the voice of God! Alas, it is the mercy of God addressing me by my name. Noah gathered himself to reply: "Yes, God!" He lisped the name of God: "Adonai Elohenu!" It was a blessing. God was speaking to him in the recognisable voice of Shem at last, in the voice of his own first-begotten son. He was calling him.

"Noah!" That was Shem! That was actually Shem's voice. Where was he? He was in the church. He had fallen from the roof! Noah sat up. He hurt himself straight off. Astonishing! In the hollow of his thigh every nerve reported with a great clatter that he was dislocated. Hell, I am in the choir, and I can't stand the pain! Somehow I must lie down. Somebody help! He got ready to whimper for help when worse happened. Noah was not alone. He knew without any shadow of doubt the presence of the lion which couched beside him. His body stretched itself in such a misery of horror then, that his bones clicked back into place, and fused solid. He was bedded down with a full-grown lion. May it have eaten! Sorrow overcame Noah.

"Well?" they all said together.

Shem shook his head. "He doesn't answer."

"We must all go down there and look for him."

"It's too dangerous."

"Surely, we must try and get him out."

"I tell you," said Shem, "you can't see a thing."

"We could make flaming torches," suggested Happoo.

"You don't understand. The animals will attack. They are at least as hungry as we are. You would need a big bonfire to keep them off. We would burn the Ark down. We can't risk a fire."

"Unless you build it in the font," said Cordelia.

"Yes! The stone font! Quick!" Ham unscrewed the oil lamp and soaked the tablecloth. "Break up some chairs or something, can't you? We need lots of wood."

"There are some sacks over there." In a very short time the family had gathered every stick of fuel in the chamber, and filled two sacks.

"Where are you going?" asked Shem.

"It's my turn," said Ham, screwing up the tablecloth as he made for the stairs. "You must all stand inside the door until you see a light, and then come at once with the wood. Happoo can guard the door. Matches!" He pocketed them.

"Wait," said Cordelia. "Hold out your hand." She took the lid off the pepper carton, and shook a handful into his palm.

"In case of wolves," he said, and ran down below. Happoo went next, then the other men with the wood. The women followed slowly. Happoo opened the door. "Wow, what a fug!" Ham disappeared.

The stone font was at the back of the nave, in the middle. There were cattle in the way. Ham elbowed them aside and rushed into the darkness. He skidded into the font step. He couldn't wait. There was something sitting on the font cover. He bent down and flung his powder, and then heaved up the cover like a shield. Whatever it was coughed with the cough of a tiger and moved lazily off. Ham threw the cover after it, and hoped there were no snakes in the font. He lit a match, and set fire to the tablecloth.

When they saw light explode the brothers ran out and built a feverish pyramid of wood. The flames leapt in the bowl, crackled and roared upwards to the vault of the church. The place was alive with light and enormous shadows, and a multitude of animals stampeding from the blaze, whisking into the pews, and leaving the back of the church to Noah's family. The women stood at the door of the newel stairs. In the firelight the animation of the men as they piled the fuel looked like an antique dance. Jemima picked her way carefully through the dirt and joined them. Then the others came, and finally Happoo, leaving the door ajar, ran across. She clutched Cordelia and pointed down the nave.

"There!"

He had laid his head upon the deck which he had made with such snug and secret joints. Beneath him the flood, the primeval ocean, ran with the thunder of whales. Beside him the lion ruled; and every breath he took was emphatic with the coarse odour of his royal neighbour. When light came, the lion raised himself couchant and regardant. But Noah lay still and looked sideways along the floor. The light was reflected in his sad eyes.

"Is he alive?"

"I can't bear to look!"

"Yes, he is alive. He is looking at us," said Kezia.

"No; he is so still. I'm afraid there is nothing we can do."

"We must!"

"If we try and move in, the lion will simply pick him up and walk off. He won't be separated from the prey. If Noah is alive, the only chance he has is to get up and run."

"Perhaps he is injured."

"If he is alive, he is probably helpless with fear."

They looked with dismay at their father. "He would never reach us, anyway," said Ham. "It is too far. Savage, isn't it?"

"He is alive! Look; he blinked."

"But he is too afraid even to speak! Look." A great tear glistened in Noah's eye, rolled over his nose, and dripped on to the chancel floor.

"This is too terrible. It is like a mouse. We must save him."

"Come here, all of you," said Cordelia, "and stand where he can see you."

Noah saw them, then, a family group, standing in their clearing of the forest, with the smoke rising, Indians in the paradise of Eden. He saw Cordelia with her arms raised above her head waving gracefully to him, and he could smell the smoke of their pyre. He lay still. There was nothing he could dare to do but weep for himself. He saw them, and then they were gone, and the flames of their camp-fire rose and fell.

Quinah! He recited the prayer of Jonah in his extremity: "Into the deep, into the heart of the seas! The flood was round about me; all thy waves and thy billows passed over me. The waters closed in over me, the deep was round about me; weeds were wrapped about my head, at the roots of the mountains." He thought, I cannot move a finger, but that prayer is a fake, Jonah's prayer from the belly of the fish! Listen to it. These words have been composed in idle security! It has all been written by a man glowing with the thought that he is back on dry land again. It is a man remembering a near squeak. It is poetry which actually celebrates the fear of death by being eaten alive! Inside his horrible head, Noah was not paralysed. He was working. His brains were whizzing along. Given the slightest shift of circumstances in his favour, an escape route could be computed like lightning. Surely he could out-think the elementary equipment of lions? He must.

He lay like a corpse, and considered frantically: It is not the afterthoughts of Jonah, it's what he actually prayed down there in the belly of the fish – that's what we want to know! What did he utter – as he was slipping down the red lane? Was it like this? What has happened to the family? There can be only one prayer which handles this extremity. It is the prayer of Jesus. It is: *Eloi, Eloi, lama sabachthani,* my God, my God, why hast thou forsaken me?

Uttered in conscious terror! He was unable to move. But his mind was working at full throttle also. So it must be inappropriate simply to register the words of Jesus as a wail of despair. There must be a way of dealing with lions. His thinking would have been as fast and concentrated. It would have been the liveliest thing that could be thought by a man full of grace. What was it?

Purring started from the lion. Noah attended to the note. If it turned into snoring, the log which was dressed in a cassock would crawl up the nave to the fire. Who, after all, would fancy a black crocodile which had been lying in manure?

If Jesus was saying something with all the calmness and clear-headedness of which he was then capable, and saying it loud, why did they confuse it? Who could think he was shouting for Elijah to let down his chariot from heaven to save him? Yet someone did. Someone thought it was just an old-fashioned cry for help. And even the gospels make different claims about what he was shouting. Why do they garble it?

Noah felt the weight of the lion resting against him. He had become a pillow for the animal's head. He shrank into the shelter of his thoughts to lock himself away from the wild signals from the muscles in his back. He expected to ripple from head to foot, and to pour out an odour of defeat and unsettle the beast sufficiently to bite its pillow into quietness.

"Into thy hands I commend my spirit." That's how Luke rattled it off. And John, what John put was: Finished! With these sayings, they both hope to clarify; but the darker sentence is nearer home: Why hast thou forsaken me? Three ways of saying the same thing, d'you think? Admit that *Eloi, Eloi lama sabachthani* is misleadingly doleful, wouldn't you try to rephrase it somehow? If you believed as Luke did that the most important thing at the death of Jesus was his serenity and confidence, that his submission was voluntary, that he was not bound by cowardice, that he didn't cling to every instant for the prickling possibility of escape, wouldn't you begin to reconstruct his bewildering cry? How can My God! My God! be understood undramatised by terror? How can it be said aristocratically, courteously, without a trace of nervousness?

Noah thought: I would like Elijah to come now – please! There is no way out of here. I want to be excused! How did Jesus ever say: It is finished, without meaning I've had enough of this, and don't want any more, and must get out? But it is simply said. It is graceful, and perfect, and goes beyond the superficial horror of being forsaken and in the dark. It is complete. It is not like this, being stuck helplessly under a lion.

Noah's heart was beating so loudly in his ears that he grieved; if the lion hears it, he will eat it!

Eloi, Eloi lama sabachthani – said with the sort of poise which Luke gives to his version, and with the finality indicated by John? Not a hopeless question full of astonishment about being deserted by God, but altogether more serious, open and deliberate, as if a philosopher on his afternoon walk had reached a point when the mysterious emptiness of religion and the meaninglessness of death held his attention entirely; not an academic question, but detached, professional: why is the absence of God essential to mortality?

It is not an issue of faith and unbelief, as if Jesus were being put to a final test excruciatingly. For he trusts God. It is that confidence which allows the question to come out at last into the open. Now the question is wide open; that is an achievement. The question is perfect because it prescribes no limit to what may be asked about God. That which forsakes the questioner is every preliminary, limited image of God, every demand that what is infinite should be less than itself even in its infinite humility and homeliness. And yet it is a terrible moment, irreversible, plunging into an abyss. It is not, why have you forsaken me but I'm all right. The process of dying advances in a tumult. Don't smell me, lion! I am awful. I am all mingled with gall!

Noah would have shouted then, under the carnivorous weight, that he was unable to penetrate the question, and had got no further than being certain of the dismal absence of God, and that nausea was the only prayer he had, when the purring of the lion stopped dead, like a time-bomb. The last little security left him. It was the end. He opened his eyes. His mouth was dry. He had a deep thirst for the flood. The lion stood up and growled. Very quietly and gently a large laundry basket descended and came to earth at the foot of the chancel steps. Noah considered it. Three ropes were attached to it. They were bell-ropes, because the sallies were in view. The middle rope was vertical; the other two went up diagonally into the dark. It was barely three steps to this machine.

There was only one thing to do; count ten and run for it. Noah felt ill. It was impossible. He was no more than a cocoon. He counted to three and his heart failed him. He looked wistfully. He had surrendered too far back to be accessible now. Then the organ spoke. Kezia was pumping the handle like a mad woman, and Cordelia brought her hands down on to every key she could reach. She turned it into the thunder of *Wachet Auf*. She opened the swell, and wept, and trod upon all the pedals of wrath. A look of sheer bewilderment came upon the face of the beast. Into the basket, without ceremony, Noah fled, his feet going like a hermit-crab, his arms flapping round the middle rope. He was raised. By a series of swift jerks, he ascended into the dark sky. My father, my father! The chariot of Israel and the horsemen thereof! He went up like a ghost to the rafters, with the help of three pulleys, three sons hauling, and the song:

> Come forth ye virgins wise:
> The Bridegroom comes, arise!
> Alleluia!

where he was carefully unloaded, carried home, helped out of his stinking cassock, and put to bed.

The chancel stood empty. A fox looked out from the top of the pulpit steps, went back in again, then ran down and sniffed among the broken egg-shells. The ashes in the font glowed and were not comprehended. Above the dog-fox the heavenly basket was moored, and swung with the barely perceptible swell of the flood.

VI

THE PIGEON ON THE WINDOW-SILL

There was a knocking. It was not the door. It sounded like workmen in the scaffolding. It was hammer and cold chisel. Tap, tap, tap. Noah sighed. He was conscious of neglecting the parish to build the Ark. It was addictive. The embarrassing thing was how the parish encouraged his devotion to the fabric, when it was such plain lust in him. Nevertheless, his first thoughts in the morning were, as usual, the day's building schedule. They were early to work today, weren't they? What job were they on now?

He opened his eyes. Someone was standing on a chair at the belfry window. It was Ham. Sunlight was streaming in.

"Try not to make too much noise." That was Cordelia's voice.

He focused his eyes beyond the foot of the bed on the bell-wheel, and the stay made from a piece of ash wood which rose from the headstock of the bell. The garterhole in the bell-wheel was empty. The bell-rope should come through there. The rope was missing. Without the rope you couldn't raise the bell. The whole nerve of the machinery was absent, the spring, the motive of the wheel. The lack of a rope's tautness in the works gave the bell a dull, hunched and definitely immobile, settled air. Instead of looking as if it could go round, the wheel stood spread-eagled by its spokes. How stationary! One of the obvious jobs must be to fix that bell. What had happened?

"Good morning."

"It is Sunday," said Noah; "why are they working on a Sunday?" He was dreaming.

Cordelia was bending over him.

"Are we late?" he began.

"Everything is all right," she said. He turned in the bed, and groaned. "It is better to lie still."

He heard himself shouting: No! No! No! No!

"Ham, come and help me," said Cordelia. They lifted Noah back.

"We shall be late for church!" he cried. "What have I done?"

"You have hurt your back. There's nothing broken, as far as we can see. You are safe. Does it hurt?"

He nodded. "Cordelia?" She knelt by the bed, and took his hand, and patted it.

"We're in the belfry, aren't we? We don't have to go to church today. Have I been asleep?"

"You've been asleep for two days. It's nice to have you back, lovey."

"I fell, you see," he confided.

"Yes."

"I fell. I've ricked my back, haven't I? We are still on the Ark."

"Yes."

"But the sun is shining. How long has the sun been out?"

"Just today, for the first time."

"Is that Ham?"

"Yes. I've knocked the louvres out of the window, so that you can have some light in here."

"What is it like?"

"What?"

"Outside."

"Marvellous; a perfectly blue sky, and just a breath of wind on the water, so that it ripples and sparkles."

The flood is shining, thought Noah.

"How are the children?"

"Fine."

"They rescued me. You all did."

"Of course."

"Why the belfry?"

"So you could be quiet. When you are better you can come downstairs again."

"If I don't move, it doesn't hurt. It is a strict sort of bed!"

"It's some of the straw, made into a mattress. Underneath that is the kitchen table. Bit hard, I'm afraid, but it's best."

"Smells nice," said Noah.

Cordelia watched his white face until his eyes closed. The dark under his eyes, and the great pinched nose, and the staring beard held her attention. She had watched all the time by his bed, the waxy skin of his forehead, the hollow cheek, looking narrowly for stages in the moribund declension of Noah. He was ageing and wearing out. His mouth went slack and his hand dropped out of hers. She studied his breathing. The strain was leaving his face. His pulse was good.

She went with Ham and stood by the high window. The roof-shingles were steaming, drying in the sun. The sea was brilliant to the horizon.

"We could all go swimming!" said Ham.

"I don't know. The water will be deadly cold. And how are you going to get back on board?"

"Mother!"

"I'm sorry. Gosh, you know, I'm tired."

"If the fine weather continues, Shem says we ought to try and give the animals a clean out. They are quite tame, really. I don't know what we were all worrying about. That lion hasn't got a mean thought in him."

"It's different when the sun shines, I agree."

"How is he?"

"Noah? I don't know. When he was lying there just now, I could hardly recognise him. Do you know that transparency of the skin? We just have to wait."

"I'll get one of the girls. It's time you had a breather."

"I'm all right."

"Come on." She looked back at the bed, and the motionless bell-wheels, and climbed down.

"We thought of sunbathing on the roof," said Happoo.

"One of you had better sit by the old man. Who's coming for a swim?"

"Thank you for tidying up," said Cordelia. "It's very nice in here."

"How is he?"

Cordelia put up her feet on the sofa. "He woke up for a little while. He asked after you all." She was crying now, copiously. Happoo went red, and hid her face in Cordelia's lap. The girls gathered round. The window of the ringing room opened, and a foot came over the sill.

"I say, you chaps," said Japheth, climbing in, "how's this?" He turned back to the window and drew in his brown line hand over hand. He held up the tackle with the weight at the

H

bottom, and displayed five fish on the hooks. "Gorgeous food!"

"What are they?"

"I would like to think they were mackerel. But I'm afraid they are only carp," he grinned.

"They're very small!"

"Don't be hard on them. They've done their best. Where's the frying pan?"

"How shall we divide them?"

"Soup would be best," said Jemima.

"Sardine soup?"

"A delicacy, an invalid's broth!"

"It would go furthest," explained Jemima. "Let me do it."

She went to the cupboard. There were herbs, basil, thyme, fennel. There was nutmeg, a clove of garlic, and a bottle of communion wine retrieved from the sacristy, two gull's eggs, olive oil, peppercorns, salt, a piece of cheese, potatoes, old bread. Sanctuary wine! If the church had stocked a decent bottle of white, that would be different.

She cleaned the fish, simmered them whole in water with enough thyme not to drown the flavour of the carp, sliced in five potatoes, and when they were ready, she took out the fish, separated the flesh from the skin and bones, and returned the flesh to the broth. She tasted it to see if there was enough salt in, and added nutmeg. In three-quarters of an hour it was ready, and the family exclaimed in gratitude for the smell. No one would eat until Noah had been served, and they all followed Jemima upstairs to where Kezia sat, aware of their hollow stomachs, to see if their father would break his fast.

He smiled at his family. How shy and small he looked! They raised him with care on the pillows. He went white and his eyes shone with fright. Kezia wiped the beads of sweat.

"Breakfast time," said Jemima. He shook his head.

"How nice of you all – to come and see me."

"A nice lazy time you're having," said Shem.

"I hope you will soon be better," Happoo clasped her hands.

"You are looking very well," said Japheth.

"He's had a nice long sleep. Try and eat a little, now."

Noah looked reluctantly at the tureen. "What is it?"

"Very special!"

He was fed like a child. The family leaned upon the bell-frames and watched intently.

"More?"

He nodded. He was ravenous. It was delicious.

"Would this be a fish soup?"

"Freshly caught."

"How clever you are." He paused only momentarily from the serious business, there was even a little colour in his cheeks. The tureen was soon half empty.

Jemima encouraged him. He lay back on the pillows.

"I'm sure I must have had my ration. Quite delicious."

"We have eaten," she said simply.

"Well, just a little."

Cordelia caught the look of consternation in Ham's eye. So did his wife. Happoo made a blissful face, and shook some sense into him. "What a banquet," she said firmly. They all laughed and Japheth went round chiming the bells.

"You'll have to finish it off. I couldn't," said Noah at last.

Cordelia gave them each a piece of bread. They dipped in turn patiently, lovingly, in the dish, with the thanksgiving of wolves. "The old devil!" said Ham as he went downstairs, "I thought he would scoff the lot."

"Plenty more," said Japheth, baiting the hooks with potato skins.

"What is it?" Noah held his wife's hand.

"Lumbago, I expect, or a slipped disc, or just a nasty bump."

"It tweaks me. I am a victim of my own vainglory."

"It was an accident."

"A judgement."

"How can you be expected to think straight if you are not very well? The only judgement you need bother about is that your wife and family don't think you are too bad, and will put up with a little inconvenience!"

"Help me," he whispered. "I am feeling sorry for myself."

"It is all right," she said kindly. "We belong together. We have always been ready to participate in your talent and success. Don't keep us out now."

"It is not my back that is wounded."

Cordelia had not shriven a priest before. But she sat holding his hand, and heard his confession.

"I am afraid of the dark, and of the abyss, and I claimed to serve God only in my strength. I am a ravening Pharisee, persistently bent upon religion, used to being élite, ambitious and smarter than the rest. I am used to being condemned out of the gospels for hypocrisy, but I go on demanding to be accepted for my merit. I despise weakness in myself, and test myself against my fears. I invest the darkness with the fantasy of danger, and with a lion. I am stiff with vainglory. I fear ridicule. I expect to do battle with the wrath of God, and am bitter about the unequalness of the contest. I cannot accept the concern of my family, or dismay them as a feeble old man. I can only command their respect and admiration for my righteousness and generosity. I am a hard man aware of the fury of Christ. I feed upon praise, and my heart is blind. I expect love to be dangerous and strong, and to involve sacrifice. But I expected to win. I am ashamed."

She was being asked for ghostly comfort, and did not know how to match this sorrow. She waited a while, and then said: "What is needed is a sublime justice, a judgement that is so understanding that there is no room left for thinking it will get things wrong. People have the right to be properly known, for only then can they be properly judged. What one needs to be confident about is that all the evidence, all that a person has been, all that he ever did and suffered is entirely plain and appreciated by the judge. In a way, it was like that with the children. There was a point in their growing up when they expected from us sublime understanding, and while it lasted, it was a high expression of mutual love.

"The judgement to wish for is the judgement of one whose concern for your life is at least as thorough as your own, whose knowledge is at least as deep, and whose righteousness is so honest, that you are able to say: Thou knowest me; thou hast searched me out and known me. And then you would recognise the person you had not in your most extravagant moments claimed to be, being set at liberty within you, not having to hide any more; and that is what it is to be forgiven." She hesitated, not sure if what she was saying was either useful or true. But Noah responded with the clean gratitude of a man absolved, of a child recovered, of a dumb creature helped to escape. He kissed her, and tugged her hair, and presently forgot all about it.

But his convalescence was slow. He sat propped up, feeling useless, among the bells, for many days in the calm weather. He was listless, easily exhausted, foolishly grateful for their attention.

"One would think the animals had got it too," said Shem; "no life in them. Probably all got worms or something."

Happoo came into the ringing room with a pigeon in her hands. "The birds are all dying! Look, he was so feeble, I could just pick him up. He hadn't the strength to flap his wings. What is it?"

"They are starving, that's what it is," said Kezia.

"What shall we do? Poor little thing!"

"Take it up and show it to Noah," said Cordelia.

"It would distress him!"

"He will have to find out some time," said Shem.

Happoo climbed the stairs to the belfry. Noah was sitting in bed looking at the patch of blue sky through the window. The frown on her face, and then the quiet bird, claimed his attention.

"I don't think it's very well."

"Let me see." He put on his glasses and inspected the pigeon. It made no attempt to escape. It sat stupidly in his hand, even when he opened its beak.

"Are there more like this one?"

"I think so."

"You must try and catch them. Have the boys been cleaning out the church?"

"Oh, yes. They have been doing a marvellous job; clean straw and everything."

"If you find any dead ones, they should be burned."

"What is it?"

"Diphtheria; well, in birds, what is called roup. See that."
He pointed to the nostrils of the pigeon, full of whitish-
yellow pus. "It's in the mouth too." He sighed.

"I shouldn't have brought it," she began.

"No, leave it. It will probably die."

"Is there nothing we can do?"

He shook his head. Happoo looked so glum, that he began
inventing. "We could teach it to gargle, do you think?"

There was a clatter down the stairs. Cordelia turned round
to meet Happoo's wild rush.

"Have we got any boracic ointment?"

"I don't know. I'll look."

"Noah wants some warm water, some boracic ointment
and a straw! Oh, quickly." She ran upstairs again.

"Wait a bit, child!"

"Sorry. He says it's probably due to overcrowding, and it's
called roup, and it's infectious. And I want a box for it to live
in."

With great delicacy Noah blew a weak solution into the
nasal passage, and washed the mouth. He did this at intervals,
and watched over the bird, nursing it, and encouraging it to
feed on hard-boiled egg chopped very fine and biscuit
crumbs soaked in a little olive oil. There was very little doubt
in his mind that it would shortly expire. But he did it for
Poo's sake; and as the hours added up, and the pigeon refused
to succumb, he became more and more concerned with its
health. He discouraged the family, even on tiptoe, from
visiting. He inspected the droppings, kept everything clean
and warm, and coaxed life back into the dowdy, emaciated,
sickly bird. In a week, its eye was bright; in a fortnight it was
the sleekest member of the crew, and walked up and down

the bed, perched on bell-wheels, and flew back to Noah for regular meals.

Noah put his feet on the floor and staggered. The fat pigeon turned its beak away and stared. He was very weak. Unsteadily he shuffled towards the belfry window, put out a hand to stop himself from falling, and the pigeon flapped and came and settled on his wrist. He was too astonished to move. He straightened his back, and considered his friend *columba palumbus,* with its fine blue, grey and purple-brown, its silk green neck and white collar.

"Come, we shall go together."

It had been another clear day. Noah looked out on the flood. The indistinctness of the abyss had been sorted out. Order and colour had been separated out in creation again. God had divided the waters from the waters, the reliable ocean, the blue heaven, clothed, and in their right minds. The sun was beginning to make a bright path across the flat sea, a credible walking place for feet to tread molten fire.

"Lord, if it be thou, bid me to come unto thee on the water."

"Come."

"It is like glass," said Noah, aware that his meditation had returned to him. "Pure gold, like unto clear glass! Garnished with all manner of precious stones, jasper, sapphire, emerald, beryl, topaz, amethyst . . . and the street of the city was pure gold, as it were transparent glass . . . in the midst of the street, the tree of life, and the leaves of the tree for the healing of the nations. I can see now why Peter was able to step out of the fisherman's boat."

"When Peter was come down out of the ship, he walked on the water, to go to Jesus. But when he saw the wind boisterous, he was afraid; and beginning to sink, he cried, saying, Lord, save me."

"And immediately Jesus stretched forth his hand, and caught him," replied Noah. "I understand, sir, the faith which wavers and is recovered. I have sailed in this Petrine dark church."

"Do you think my walking on the water is just the sun's track?"

"That the miracle is a sort of insubstantial glory? I think the story was remembered because it speaks truly about the confidence and shakiness of faith."

"But the miracle itself is unimportant? Just glitter?"

"People get uneasy about miracles. It is a mad, mythological way, perhaps, of illustrating the nature of faith, all right for the evangelists . . ."

"All right aesthetically?"

"Yes." There could be no more compelling revelation than the light of the throne of God spreading upon the crystal water.

"But not something that happens. Try once more. Put the pigeon on the window-sill. It is a beast full of eyes, isn't it? It will do for an evangelist. Stand behind him. Can you see over his shoulder?"

"Yes."

"You can only see over an evangelist's shoulder. What do you see?"

"The sun on the water. It is towards evening."

"Suppose there is a fishing boat out there."

"Where?" He bent down to the sill and studied the calm ocean. The pigeon walked across and stood in front of his face. He smiled. "It's in the way!"

"Yes. Now much further still, beyond the boat, do you see someone walking on the water?"

"No."

"Look! In a direct line, coming towards the fishing boat."

Noah screwed up his eyes and stared. He searched to the horizon, concentrating all his desire to see. The waves were on fire, flecked with black. He was ashamed of his lack of discovery, and was dying to say – yes! As he went carefully over the same area again and again, inspecting the same empty sea, recognition came. He stood up quite calmly. "But you are here, Lord!" he said.

"Yes. It is simple. The miracle is not something curious about my specific gravity. It is what relates you and me."

Noah understood. "After all, how could I know you – at such a distance, across so endless a flood? You are the man who suffered under Pontius Pilate!"

"So it is a miracle how I reach you. But nothing can separate us, and not ever so much water. Love unites instantaneously. Like the way the story is in the fourth gospel – "It is I; do not be afraid. Then they were ready to take him aboard, and immediately the boat reached the land they were making for!"

Noah held up his hand against the western sun. He looked away. Then once more he stared at the horizon beneath the reddening sky. He picked up the pigeon, and crossed the belfry in no time.

"Gangway!" he roared, "I'm coming down. Cordelia! Shem! Where are you. Summon all hands!"

"Darling, do be careful!" Bare feet came down the rungs fast.

Noah stood before them in his nightie, with the pigeon on his shoulder.

"You are better!"

"That is nothing. Go and look at the sea, in the direction of the sun, without dazzling your eyes. Don't make up your minds too quickly."

They crowded the window.

"Well?" he asked patiently.

"Islands!" said Happoo.

"Icebergs," said Ham.

"I thought of that."

"Whales, it could be whales basking," said Shem.

"Or seaweed."

"Is it . . ." Cordelia began to ask.

"It is the tops of mountains!" said Noah, as if it were his birthday.

"I say, you chaps," said Japheth, "shall we ring the bells?"

"From now on," said Jemima, "we shall need a look-out up there. I don't know about ringing the bells."

When the water was receding, and the mountains rose sheer out of the water, before there was any land or slope to perch on, Noah sailed among the fjords between the great peaks. It was silent. His friends were all gone under the sea, and lay at the bottom of the mountains on the floor of the world. He had thought: it will be clear to the bottom. There will be the lost cities and bell-towers below. But the waters of the fjord were impenetrable night. He sailed over no market-places, nor cathedrals. He did not see his friends; only the reflection of the wooden church, and his own face gliding over the standing flood.

He took his pigeon on the fist, went to the window, and let him fly.

"Have you ever realised what eyes pigeons have," he explained. "Watch that bird. When you compare the eyes to the rest of the anatomy of the skull, they are immense."

"It is circling."

"It is returning."

Noah put out his hand and took the bird in to him into the Ark. "It means there is nowhere to land yet." He smiled: "This is a clever bird."

But they knew the journey was coming to an end. And in the evenings, Jemima appeared in her best clothes, and spent a good deal of time combing her hair, as if she was going to meet someone.

"How brown you all look," said Cordelia.

"Weather-beaten!" said Kezia.

"It will be nice to eat something other than fish," said Ham.

"Would you like to play cards?" asked Happoo.

"As for that," Shem turned to Noah, "you never did tell us what you had thought about the walking on the water."

"It has something to do with eternity," said Noah.

"What?"

"About time and distance not being all that important," he continued. "Do you know, once when we were in Worm-easter, some people came after dark, anxious to look at the church? I didn't want to disappoint them, so I went to unlock the place for them. How long I crouched in front of the door feeling for the keyhole only those people will remember. It was a very black night. It took a long time, because in fact the door was wide open. We were gathered in the darkness around an obstacle that didn't exist. It is remarkable to feel the resistance of an invisible door! I suppose we tumbled into the nave like sheep, and could only tell the inside from the echo, and from a slight exhilaration in the heart which marked the discovery that one was unable to say where was the threshold between the darkness and the darkness.

"Eternity is like that. It is like someone leaving the door open. And there is no problem, really.

"I suppose the trouble is that we think God has to do with eternity in a grand, inhuman way, as primordial as the flood. But if he loves us, and if it is real love, the way we love one another here, the way you affect me indelibly, then for all his eternity he has, in precisely the same way, to belong to us. And if it is eternity, and not a temporary thing that is bound to decay, if it is all present to him, then the fact that we have made an impression on God can never be lost."

"I don't know if I have understood," said Happoo with a serious face.

"It is difficult to put into words." There was a clatter on the window-sill.

"What's that?"

"It is the pigeon come back," replied Noah, standing in the evening light.

"Oh look! In its beak, a leaf!"

"An olive leaf," said Cordelia.

"Plucked off."

When the water drained away, Noah expected, he would walk through cities of petrified, antediluvian men, in sunlight, as through the halls of the dead, observing the sea-change, and the gear covered with barnacles. In fact, when the waters were dried from off the earth, in the first month, the first day of the month, there was mud as far as the eye could see.

Noah looked both ways, rolled up his trousers, and walked barefoot, careful of his back, testing the blue mud. He sang a song of praise to God for covering the bones with such a fine sediment. "*Et lux perpetua luceat eis,*" he sang, uncertainly. His family were having a picnic higher up the beach. They looked well but famished. He broke off the surface of mud where it was cracked and worked it in his fingers as he had seen Coombes the farmer do. In the imagination of his heart, he saw it growing many things.